The Genie Who Had Wishes of His Own

To Dr. Harpster,
a professional genie!

Margaret Harmon

The Genie
Who Had Wishes
of His Own

21st-Century
Fables

Margaret Harmon

PLOWSHARE MEDIA
LA JOLLA, CALIFORNIA

ISBN: 978-0-9821145-8-2
Library of Congress Control Number: 2013941631

All illustrations by the author
Photo of the author by Fritz Harmon

Published by Plowshare Media, P. O. Box 278, La Jolla, CA 92038

PLOWSHAREMEDIA.COM
MARGARETHARMON.COM

For Ronal Kayser

Preface

Fables speak truth in a murky world. They help us make our lives work: become our favorite self, find love, be healthy, make our fortune, see how life really works. We may have to reread a fable, analyze it, sleep on it, discuss it with friends—but at its core is fearless truth.

Humans have been writing fables for 3,000 years in every culture—new ones each time the culture changes. Why? Because they're efficient. Better than a lecture doling out facts and figures, a fable is a *story*, so we live the hero's life through our five senses. We understand and believe and remember ... because we are there.

A fable explores a philosophy of life by having a character live it 100% so we see the consequences. King Midas—granted his wish that *everything* he touches will turn to gold—is delighted when furniture, books, and a rose turn to gold. But when he hugs his daughter, she hardens in his arms into solid gold. Doomed to carry greed to its logical extreme, Midas loses his daughter so we can save ours.

It's interesting to debate a fable's meaning. Though we all read the same words, we each read our own fable—a literary Rorschach. And as we mature, fables deepen with us. We see what we're ready to see.

My fables—like Aesop's originally—don't end with didactic morals. (Victorians added the morals when they selected certain fables for children and wanted to make sure kids got the message.) Aesop wrote for adults, who took pride in figuring out a fable's meaning.

Heroes battling our personal dragons are the favorites we carry with us, warning us away from dangerous habits, inspiring us to *do* what fulfills us. Villains we recognize are precisely the enemies we want to understand.

Like very rich chocolates, fables are best savored one at a time.

ACKNOWLEDGMENTS

Many people's intelligence helped shape this book. Bette Blaydes Pegas, Dorothy Ledbetter, and Judy Barkley have read re-re-rewrites without losing patience or focus.

Ronal Kayser, Carol Ryrie Brink, Barnaby Conrad, and Ray Bradbury shared wisdom they spent their lives developing.

Wayne, Andrea, and Fritz Harmon are the honest readers I couldn't do without. I thank Beth and David Singer, Betty Imlay, Ann Wolfensberger, Maxine Seltzer, and Jim Coatsworth for their expertise, and Ralph Cates, Larry Edwards, Tim Brittain, and Plowshare Media for their commitment to publishing *The Genie Who Had Wishes of His Own*.

CONTENTS

One Piece of Perfection 1

The Ladder 15

The Ingénue & the Genie 21

The Song Sparrow 29

The Artist 37

The Woman Who Loved Her Husband 53

The Philanthropist 63

The Great Zapizzis 77

Freeing the Genie 85

The Well Digger 93

Fairhaven 97

Two Young Farmers 121

The Second-best Juggler in the World 131

The Dog Who Won the Right to Bite 139

The Snake in the Terrarium 147

The Woman & Her Spring 151

The Caterer's Daughter 155

Rex 167

The Track Team 177

A Bite of Toast 183

The Caterpillar 189

The Captain's Table 195

One Piece
of
Perfection

An idealistic young architect named Zoe knew a hundred professionals who wanted to live downtown in a port city, but there was no chic housing downtown. She realized that if she designed a ten-story building of forty condominiums—architecturally striking and high-tech with green construction—she could establish herself as a design pioneer and help her friends live really well without destroying the Earth.

"Put in $60,000 cash with a mortgage of $300,000," she said, "and you'll have a condo worth five times as much to you—you'll see—while reducing your carbon footprint five sizes."

She put her own life savings in first, and thirty-nine artists, attorneys, doctors, professors, and business owners each paid $60,000 down and watched the building grow.

Choosing an award-winning contractor and the very latest technology to make her building earthquake-safe, fireproof, termite-resistant, solar-powered, solar-tube-lit, and equipped with a wind-driven air conditioning system of her own invention, she built it eleven stories tall, to make room for a gym and eco-batteries on the ground floor. Underground parking provided two spots for each condo plus twenty spaces for guests. A rain- and fog-catching system on the roof produced water pure enough to drink.

The condos were so eco-friendly, energy-efficient, and inexpensive to live in that Zoe called them "econdos." The building was so beautiful from every angle that she named it *Belle Maison*.

Owners met monthly for potluck suppers to learn about her inventions and bond with each other. They appreciated how cleverly she had positioned their building on the lot to give each condo a view of the bay, ocean, city skyline, or mountains. Every balcony had a solar barbeque to avoid charcoal's carcinogens. All window screens were magnetically charged to collect particles so air passing through them carried no pollen or soot.

The econdos were identical inside because the prices were identical—and because Zoe designed the structure in precise geometric units that interlocked to provide absolute structural integrity. They were airy and sunlit, with a floor plan so functional that furniture and art settled in to express each owner's personality as though the spaces had been individually designed.

Belle Maison provided all the energy its residents used. The roof and south-facing wall were solar tiled, and the gym's exercycles, treadmills, and weight machines turned electric generators. The elevator used electricity to ascend, but recharged its battery as it descended. Wind turbines on each corner of the building actually earned money for the owners. Their city was periodically buffeted by storms from the sea and, during severe winds, the wind turbines automatically adjusted to catch more wind and create more electricity. Turning the turbines dissipated the force of the wind, and the grateful city paid a small fee whenever wind speed rose above thirty knots.

Owners greeted each other in elevators and stairwells as partners sharing a whole greater than its forty parts. They had no power bills, low water bills, and air so clean they dusted their furniture only twice a year.

As word of Belle Maison's beauty and energy efficiency spread, international media lionized Zoe. After appearing on the covers of seventy-three magazines in sixteen countries, she sold her beloved econdo to a red-haired interior designer living one floor above her and moved to Paris, where she was commissioned to design *Belles Maisons II et III.*

The econdo owners lived Zoe's idealism and maintained

their homes in perfect harmony ... until a hairy-armed CEO in a west-facing condo tired of his ocean view because "at night a dark ocean is boring." Extending his balcony just three feet would give him the city skyline and lots of lights. He had the maintenance crew from his company push heavy-duty railing out three feet and add sturdy flooring.

When a writer who had turned her living room into her studio without changing any walls confronted the CEO about risking Belle Maison's structure by enlarging his balcony, he told her, "My condo is *my* condo" and slammed the door on her shoe.

A therapist with a mole on her lip tired of being perpetually cold. She called a builder to glass in her balcony so she could enjoy sun without wind. The builder suggested making it five feet longer and ten feet wider to create a solarium. The therapist bought furniture for her new room and began growing orchids.

But her solarium shaded the balconies below it, so a history professor extended his balcony ten feet, widened it fifteen feet, and planted palm trees in its corners. A ballerina kept her balcony small, but was angry. She had converted her living room into a ballet studio—with mirrored wall, barre, and hardwood floor—while maintaining Zoe's perfect design.

An attorney whose hobby was architecture sued the owners of the three extended balconies. "Belle Maison is a living work of life-sustaining art. Hodge-podging it destroys its value. We didn't buy concrete, steel, and glass; we bought a concept, design, and beauty that belongs to all of us."

The judge decreed that, as a work of art as well as a life-sustaining home owned by all, Belle Maison could not have its balconies modified. But since the building was not designated as a historic landmark with preservation orders, he couldn't force the removal of what was already done. He could only stop further desecration of the exterior.

That winter a wine-connoisseur banker hired a specialist who combined hypersonic jackhammering with concrete acid etching to secretly carve a walk-in wine cellar from the six-foot-thick concrete wall between his condo and the elevator shaft.

The operatic tenor next door found out and hired the specialist to excavate a soundproof practice studio from his wall of the elevator shaft.

An artist had two friends help him convert his condo into a loft space by stealthily removing all interior walls and suspending his bed from the ceiling. A harpist replaced her interior walls with glass bricks, for more light and brighter acoustics.

An English teacher had her out-of-work brother replace her condo's inside walls with bookcases accessible from both sides.

An orthopedic surgeon on the top floor planted fruit trees on the roof. Their fruit was delicious, but they shaded the solar panels and their leaves clogged the wind turbines and rainwater collector.

The red-haired interior designer who'd bought Zoe's econdo one floor beneath hers hired a contractor to remove the floor/ceiling between the two living rooms to create a two-story Great Room with stained glass in all the windows. It took the contractor a year to blast, drill, and saw through four feet of concrete and rebar. When the ballerina said it was dangerous to tear out bearing walls and ceilings and floors, the interior designer said, "Mind your own business."

Three years later, a seismic tremor rattled the port city. Belle Maison residents didn't worry because Zoe had made their building earthquake proof. But the tremor hit a frequency that made Belle Maison sway. Enlarged balconies exaggerated its sway and the trees extended its arc.

The trees slid off the roof. The heavy solarium and extended balconies yanked their condos from the building and flung them to the sidewalk. Appliances shot from holes in walls. Stained glass windows popped out of the two-story great room bulging into the street. Glass bricks exploded into shards. Elevator cables snapped and the elevator free fell into the parking garage as its shaft collapsed into the wine connoisseur's cellar and tenor's studio, crushing the artist's loft and English teacher's house of bookcases.

On the ninth floor, the writer who'd kept her econdo walls as Zoe had designed them, heard creaks and small explosions.

She crouched behind her sturdy sofa, as advised by disaster survival manuals.

But she didn't need to. Her econdo, a precise geometric unit of reinforced concrete and steel, rode down through Belle Maison like an elevator car, landing on the rubble of the condos weakened by their owners. So did the ballerina's and twenty-seven other econdos remaining as Zoe had built them. Surrounded by the rubble of lesser-built neighbor buildings, twenty-nine econdo cubes rested on eleven crushed like beer cans.

The ballerina and writer telephoned Zoe in Paris, and when she saw news footage of the disaster she returned immediately to Belle Maison with sketchbook and drawing pencils. The owners of the twenty-nine surviving econdos met with her to see if Belle Maison could be rebuilt.

Zoe opened the meeting with a smile. "A problem inspires its own solution."

An attorney sat forward. "Rebuilding is pointless if greedy people can destroy it again. We need tougher contracts."

A blonde biologist nodded. "Humans are acquisitive and competitive. Many animals are. But do humans lack a sense of 'enough'?"

A psychiatrist adjusted his glasses. "Some of us don't *get* the impact of our actions."

A museum director twisted her heavy bronze necklace. "Possessions express our personalities, but Belle Maison provides excellent space for self-expression."

An engineer cleared his throat. "G + I > W = Kablooey. If Greed plus Ignorance are greater than Wisdom, we'll destroy the planet and, of course, ourselves."

A statistician spoke from the back of the room. "Only 47.6% of humans are smart enough to appreciate Belle Maison, while just 18.4% have the self-discipline to sustain it."

"Eighteen percent!" Zoe's stomach dived under her belt buckle. "Only eighteen percent?"

Finally, the writer said, "*We* want Belle Maison. Let's rebuild it for *us*. When people see how well we're living, they'll build their own Belles Maisons everywhere."

All but two surviving owners voted to rebuild Belle Maison and sign a contract promising not to damage any safety or eco features. The two dissidents cashed out their insurance settlements and moved away, and their econdos were bought by a gentle pediatrician and a wise oceanographer.

Adding her European earnings to the remaining settlements, Zoe built thirty new econdos in a ten-story building with a carbon fiber elevator in a titanium shaft. Combining the space that had been the wine connoisseur's condo and the therapist's, she built a greenhouse where econdo owners could grow organic vegetables year round. The English teacher's condo was replaced by a library. The artist's loft became an art gallery. The tenor's condo was now a lovely small theater.

Zoe invented a movable wall to give owners greater

design and function flexibility. Each living room ceiling was now supported by a carbon steel post to which she attached a wall that could swing ninety degrees to enlarge one room and shrink another.

For the new staircases, she created pressure-sensitive piezoelectric steps so people recharged Belle Maison's batteries whenever they walked up or down stairs.

Each new econdo was a precise geometric unit of concrete and steel, interlocking, balanced, divinely proportioned. Zoe rebuilt her original unit, replacing the space above it with an interfaith chapel/meditation room and labyrinth, in gratitude to all the owners who fulfilled themselves without endangering others.

She wrote a Construction Code and Owners' Manual explaining how every design and functional element interacted, and her attorney wrote a contract for owners promising to protect Belle Maison. Residents formed a Committee of Owners empowered to oversee changing anything bigger than a light bulb; the writer and ballerina co-chaired it.

Zoe watched happily as all the owners signed their final contract—until a software designer muttered and balked. When he finally signed the document, his hand shook, smearing his signature, and he growled as he left the room. Zoe followed him outside. "Why?" she asked.

The software designer glared. "Who *are* you people, to tell us how to live?"

Zoe kept her voice calm. "Why do you live in Belle

Maison if you don't like it?"

"Changing a few things won't destroy it."

"Which few—solar panels and wind turbines? The bearing walls?" Zoe felt her cheeks redden.

"Well, but..."

"But what? You'd rather drive a car as big as a house, eat food so processed it has *no* expiration date, and *hide* from sun and wind instead of *using* them?"

"Never mind," he snapped. "I'll sell!"

Zoe reached out and shook his hand.

She ran alone on the beach to think. *Are we crazy to keep fighting for Belle Maison?*

The waves rushed toward her, hissing, flattening previous waves, gliding back to sea to rise again. She ran higher on the sand to keep her shoes dry, and watched the surf. New waves rose and rushed to shore, collapsed against the sand, and slid out to sea, where they swelled again and surged ashore.

Waves recycle each other! She laughed and slowed to a walk, dodging surf that kept chasing her shoes. "And you never quit!"

A flock of seabirds flew past her. They banked and turned, flashing gray-brown backs, then white bellies, and landed at the water's edge. Dainty birds stabbed short bills into the sand for shallow crustaceans. Birds with long bills plunged them into the sand up to their eyes and brought up deep prey.

Swallows shaped like curved blades sliced the air above the kelp, capturing flies.

Zoe watched a long time.

Those who fit the earth, thrive. And those who don't… die out.

"The eighteen percent." She inhaled enough ocean air to fill herself from her shoes to her sunglasses and walked home to Belle Maison.

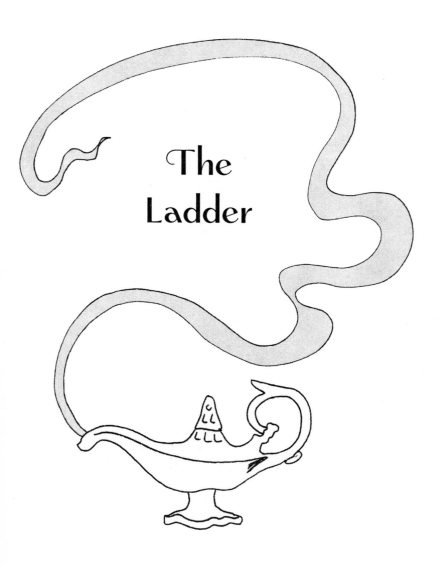

The
Ladder

A master carpenter from the city was driving his horse cart through a cobble-streeted village. When one wheel hit an oversized cobble, the carpenter's ladder bounced out of the cart. The horse's clattering hooves drowned out the ladder's clunk onto the cobblestones, and the carpenter drove on, unaware of his loss.

A peasant stumbling from the village tavern fell across the ladder, breaking a toe and bruising his knees. He struggled to his feet, spat on the ladder, and staggered away, cursing "vile logs in the middle of a street."

A second peasant saw the ladder lying in the street and

recognized its potential. He hacked a length off each leg for firewood and carried the pieces proudly home to his wife.

A third peasant, toting a bag of flour from the mill, grinned when he saw the ladder. He dragged it to the river he crossed daily on slippery rocks. Standing the ladder on one riverbank, he let it fall across to the other, making a nice little bridge. He explained the good fortune to his family at supper.

As a full moon rose above the village, a burglar crept from the forest. Fording the river on the usual stones, he saw the ladder linking bank to bank. "What's *this?*" he hissed, and snatched it up.

Tiptoeing to the finest house in the village, he leaned the ladder against its tall stone walls and climbed through a window he'd been admiring from below for years. Soon, he descended the ladder with a bulging sack over his shoulder. He pulled the ladder down after himself and hid it in a ditch.

An apprentice carpenter on his way home from work saw the ladder in the ditch and recognized it instantly as a master carpenter's ladder, with finely shaped rungs and handrails. Its feet had been chopped off unevenly, but the youth saw how to fix that. He hoisted the ladder onto his shoulders and carried it home.

He was thrilled to discover its top and bottom, front and back, and how each rung not only lifted a climber but held the two handrails together. The better he understood how the unknown master carpenter had built this ladder, the more he admired him and treasured his work.

A week later, the apprentice took the ladder apart and reassembled it. Then he built a new one that was longer and, with it, he built a house.

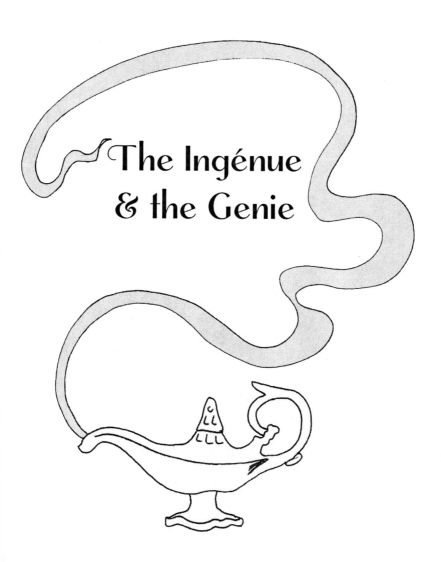

The Ingénue
& the Genie

There was once a girl named Roxanne who wanted so desperately to be a success that she could barely close her eyes at night to sleep. She watched celebrity shows and practiced being interviewed, alone in her room. In her high school yearbook, the prediction under her senior photo read, "She'll be famous."

As a college freshman she majored in American Literature to write the Great American Novel, and wrote two short stories that were published. But when she saw three movies in one weekend and realized that "Nobody's reading anymore; it's all about visuals," she changed her major to drama. During her sophomore year, a boyfriend convinced her to major in physics because she was really good in math, and beautiful women physicists grab headlines. But it took a lot more work to be *great* at physics than to be *good* at it. As a junior, she became an accounting major to make a fortune on Wall Street, but trying to never make a mistake limited her creativity. She switched to physical education to be a personal trainer in Hollywood so she could make hands-on contacts with stars, but when the novelty wore off, her classes were boring.

Interning at a New York publishing company after graduation, Roxanne spent her spare time in antique shops, searching through costume jewelry cases to find real gold, platinum, and gems that had been mislabeled. One day, in a shop with particularly interesting faux ruby brooches and wannabe emerald rings, she moved an ancient clay oil lamp off a glass case full of Art Nouveau rings and pendants. To avoid scratching the glass, she put the heavy lamp on the floor. So people wouldn't trip over it, she slid it between two bookcases. It barely fit; she had to force it with her foot.

The Art Nouveau pieces were exquisite and, as she peered through the glass at a possibly genuine emerald ring, she saw, swirling from between the bookcases, mist coagulating into a human form. Within moments, it became a slender genie with a jeweled turban.

Roxanne looked around. She was alone except for the shopkeeper waxing an armoire on the opposite side of the store.

The genie smiled and straightened his turban. "Three wishes," he said. "Anything you want."

Her heart pounded. Was this perfect or what? She swallowed hard. "*Anything?*"

The genie nodded. "That's my job."

Roxanne smiled. "I want to be a success."

"Okay." He rubbed his hands together. "As what?"

She opened her mouth... then closed it again. She inhaled. And let her breath out. "Which will be better—a film director making smash hit movies that elucidate current philosophical contradictions, or the inventor of a vaccine to prevent the Ebola virus? The vaccine is more idealistic, but I'd have to support my lab with soft money."

The genie shook his head. "I don't choose. Only grant." He smiled encouragement and crossed his arms. "This is opportunity, not necessity." He waited.

She thought until her eyes bulged.

He looked at a grandfather clock ticking near the door. "I think this shop is closing pretty soon."

Roxanne's face reddened, and tears filled her eyes.

"I'm granting you three wishes," the genie said. "Whatever you want, and you're—"

"I know." She ran her fingers through her hair. "It's just that whenever I see someone succeeding at something I could do, I stop what I'm doing and start what she's doing. I'll never succeed if I keep changing direction like this. Even talented people—"

"True," the genie interrupted. "But they're closing."

"Can you get back in there so I can carry you home on the subway? I don't think you can ride dressed in just that."

The genie frowned. "All right. But hurry. He's locking the door."

Roxanne ran to the shop owner and bought the crusty lamp. Outside in the damp air she bent over it and pretended to cough so she could whisper, "We'll be home in half an hour; I'll tell you when it's safe to come out again." On the subway, her eyes darted as she pressured herself to choose what she should succeed as.

In her tiny third-floor apartment, she set the lamp on the dining table beside her only window and called into the spout, "We're home. You can come out."

Nothing.

She called again, her stomach knotting. Had she lost her chance? Her greatest chance in the world to succeed and she'd wasted it? She shook the lamp. Turned it upside down. Tried to pull the lid off. She rubbed it.

The genie rose from the spout. "Ah yes. Your first wish is to succeed at what you'll tell me."

She took a deep breath and squeezed her eyes shut.

"Ready?" the genie asked.

"Almost," she said.

He nodded and began humming something ancient.

Roxanne paced the floor and pep-talked herself. "What am I *best* at? But this is a magic wish so I can choose *anything*, right?" She turned to the genie. "I can, can't I—wish anything I want, whether I'm gifted at it or not?"

"Certainly." He closed his eyes, swaying to the rhythm of his humming.

"Then I should go for fame and fortune. I want to be the most famous singer in the world—who earns the most money."

He opened his eyes. "Religious chanting or opera or—what type of music is popular now?"

"Oh, why not opera? But I hate opera! It's ridiculous and—" As she flung her arms, despising opera, she knocked the lamp from the table and out the window to the concrete below, where it shattered into a thousand pieces that bounced and rolled until cars ran over some and people walked on others, crushing them into the sidewalk and street.

Roxanne leaned out her window as mist rose from the gutter, floated gently toward the river, and joined a fog bank.

The Song
Sparrow

I n an oak tree, a Song Sparrow warmed up for a concert by singing deep slow tones with his eyes closed. He'd mastered his music and *lived* his technique, but he was calming his racing pulse and centering himself in that zone from which art springs.

While rabbits and deer found holes and hillocks in the clearing around the tree, an Acorn Woodpecker who was the sparrow's new assistant collected admission fees of five seeds or a small fruit.

The woodpecker flew to the branch while the sparrow was vocalizing. "Listen," he said. "Some finches are hiding in those ceanothus bushes—planning not to pay. I'll be right back; I have to drill a few heads as examples."

"Oh, I saw them fly in," the sparrow said. "But finches are enthusiastic, well-informed music-lovers who enjoy concerts so fully that they bring an audience to life and make performances magical. Let them stay."

The woodpecker shrugged and returned to collecting seeds and fruits. Soon he'd gathered so many he had to put them in storage holes in the back of a pine tree. As he tamped acorns into a row of pre-drilled holes, he overheard four Scrub Jays.

"He sings the same songs, year after year," complained one.

"Well, his interpretation offends me," sniffed the second.

"Oh, he interprets? I thought this wasn't his native language," scoffed a third, laughing so hard he had to flap his wings for balance.

"He's getting old," said the fourth. "Those high notes haven't cracked … yet. We'll see, tonight."

Stunned by their cruelty, the woodpecker darted to the sparrow's side. "I need permission to drill skulls; the jays here are—"

"I heard," interrupted the sparrow. "Rather, their vicious words roiled this air. But neither envy nor ignorance gives me information that helps me sing better. We mustn't honor them by listening."

"*Please*. Let me drill 'em."

"No. They'd get publicity they don't merit."

The woodpecker pleaded with his eyes.

The sparrow shut his with finality.

When the sparrow resumed deep breathing to block out distractions, the woodpecker floated back to the ground—but he did veer close to the jays and whir his flight feathers.

Collecting small fruits from a party of squirrels and raccoons, the woodpecker couldn't forget the jays' critique. *The sparrow is getting on in seasons. Are those high notes a little breathy? Or is this just a thought they've planted?* He shook his wings and straightened his feathers. "His interpretation is superb! He's a master, and experience deepens the well he draws from!"

He was so confused by the clash between their searing remarks and his own enjoyment of the sparrow's music that he lost track of admissions paid and those to be collected.

He groaned as a flock of Bushtits fluttered to a manzanita bush. Twittering, they traded places again and again, landing on top of each other to squeeze in where there was no room, searching for the perfect perch from which to see and hear the concert.

"Oh, stop," the woodpecker muttered. "Every perch here is excellent. It doesn't *matter!*"

But the Bushtits flitted back and forth, nudging and chittering until every animal in the clearing had exhausted the capacity to ignore them.

The woodpecker alighted beside the sparrow, who was pointing his beak skyward to stretch his throat.

33

"Lemme drill 'em," the woodpecker begged. "Just a few. Set an example."

"Heavens, no! With their metabolism, they *need* music. And I need to have my music needed." Then, with compassion for his manager's stress, "Just moments to go. They'll quiet down."

The Song Sparrow looked into the woodpecker's eyes. "We've prepared every way we can. In a minute I'll step out there and sing because I *love to sing!*"

The concert began when the sun slid behind a hill, dimming the clearing. It was the most magnificent performance of the Song Sparrow's career. The high tones were exquisitely clear; his low range had never been warmer. The sparrow sang with an intimacy that assured each creature in the audience "He's singing to *me.*"

The Bushtits settled into the shadows, inhaling and exhaling with the sparrow. The jays tilted their heads, moved deeply despite their expectations.

Squirrel parents in a front burrow held their baby up; then cuddled him with their eyes closed, rocking him to the music.

Wild applause of hooting, whistling, and chirping, with a standing ovation, brought the sparrow back for three encores. Flowers festooned his branch and blanketed the oak. He was mobbed after the concert by listeners anxious to express their joy and see him in the feather.

As the audience flew, crawled, and burrowed home, the woodpecker carried the loveliest flowers from the ground to the sparrow. "A very fine crowd," the woodpecker said. "650 seeds and 95 fruits divided by five, plus ... That's 225."

The sparrow beamed. "250, counting the finches."

The woodpecker nodded. "Did you see the jays quit whispering and nudging by the third song?"

"No," said the sparrow. "Did you see the squirrels hold up their baby? I filled him with music till his eyes bulged." His own eyes glistened.

"Well," the woodpecker said, "*The Meadowlands* critic was frowning. Wonder what he'll write. He has bizarre ideas about technique, and he's cocksure."

The sparrow closed his eyes. "Did you see the young sparrow on the center aisle, carrying his portfolio of songs? I used to do that—hoping to be asked what's in the portfolio. Ohhh, I remember. Look where it's all led." He inhaled so thoroughly the woodpecker felt his own feathers lift.

The woodpecker chuckled. "Did you see that bear fall asleep in the back—and those otters roll out of the way, then crawl up the aisle to hear *you* instead of his snoring?"

The sparrow shook his head. "Did you hear the Ornitho Cantata's arpeggios, then the plummet of trills—that complete silence when the crowd was *with* me—not one sound, not even a breath? It was *magic!* We sing for those moments. Oh, the joy of your throat full of song echoing in others' ears ... " In ecstasy, the sparrow ate a flower.

The woodpecker watched. "Why do you not see or hear the bad things? They happen; they're part of reality!"

"Because," said the sparrow, pressing tender, fragrant flowers against his throat, "I cannot *sing* in doubt and fear."

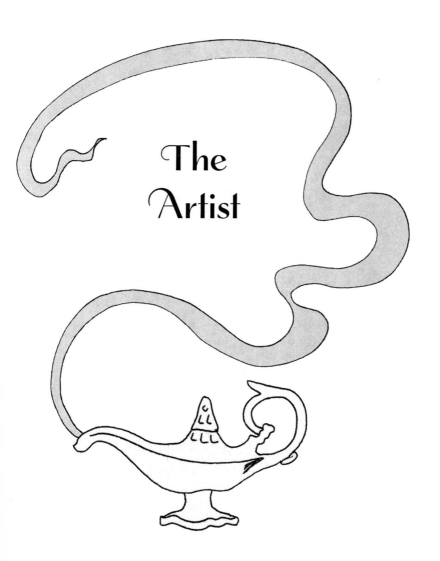

The
Artist

One Friday morning, stockbroker Ted Wood exploded at his computer. "I'm selling—to people I never see—the *hope* that numbers on my screen for *seconds* will make them money that won't vaporize before they spend it!!!" His eyes bulged and his throat closed as fellow brokers telephoned for paramedics without budging from their own screens.

Strapped onto a gurney in an ambulance swerving through traffic, Ted promised himself through the oxygen mask, "I will never set foot in that office again. I will get a real job."

The ER physician pronounced him a healthy-so-far stress victim—warning him to stop smoking, start exercising, and take a relaxation class.

Ted was so relieved to breathe on his own that he threw his Benson & Hedges in a toxic waste container and climbed the stairs to the HMO co-pay window.

That night, falling asleep, Ted tried to discover who he was. He remembered himself as Teddy, curly-haired and chubby-cheeked, his mother's favorite.

As he drifted awake in the morning, his dream refused to dissolve. He was Teddy in The Little Prince Preschool, wearing a red plastic apron, holding a long-handled paintbrush, standing at an easel he wouldn't share. His artwork was breathtakingly precocious. In fact, his mother carried it home for display on the refrigerator. She matted and framed his best work, for the family room.

He had never again felt as loved and gifted as at The Little Prince and at home in the family room. "I am," he informed his alarm clock, "an *artist*."

He enrolled that afternoon in private drawing lessons with Salvatore McInnes. In his studio McInnes had fruit, flowers, bottles, spheres, a mandolin, and his own dog, as subjects for pupils to draw.

Ted began with fruit, but McInnes couldn't tell Ted's cantaloupe from a banana. The mandolin Ted drew resembled a walrus. His flowers wouldn't bloom; his spheres sagged on the paper as flat circles. When the dog saw her portrait, she wet the floor.

"Perhaps," McInnes said kindly, "drawing is not your medium."

Ted registered for "Fundamentals of Sculpture: Clay," in a local college's extension program. He bought a red plastic apron and wore old shoes he could splash on. The first class went well—cutting clay into the model's general shape. The second did not go as well. When he returned for the third class, his sculpture's arms had dried and fallen off.

He selected a marble-sculpting course from a new instructor and purchased a block of marble. After penciling his plans onto the block, he picked up a mallet and chisel, to begin. But he smashed his thumb with the mallet—and flung his marble block to the floor, just missing the model's foot. The instructor insisted Ted leave.

In despair, Ted treated himself to an afternoon at the Municipal Museum of Contemporary Art, with a deluxe docent tour. He was amazed to hear about artists' "jokes" and the "openness" of galleries to "anything." He learned that artists "allude" to each other's works by copying bits of famous art in their own style.

He clapped his hand to his forehead. "I've been *trying* too hard!"

"What?" the docent asked.

"What *conceit*, to compete with Michelangelo!" Ted said. "I will just earn a decent living as a humble working artist." He pumped the docent's hand in gratitude and went directly to an art supply store.

Ted had noticed in the art museum that successful modern artists paint large, so he ordered a square canvas eight feet wide from the art store's Custom Desk. He bought three long-handled brushes and ten tubes of acrylic paint.

The canvas was ready in two days, and when Ted drove his convertible down to pick it up, he bought a pint bottle of Titanium White acrylic to lighten his pure, dark colors. But, maneuvering the enormous canvas through his condo doorway, he tripped on the doorstep and fell full length onto his new canvas. Worse, the pint bottle of Titanium White split open when he fell on it.

The canvas now bore a full-body impression of Ted in white acrylic. Even his teeth showed, where his face had smashed into the canvas. When he put on his glasses to see if the canvas was ripped or could still be used, he discovered tiny fibers from his clothing impressed into the paint: indigo fibers from his jeans, red and green fuzz from his flannel shirt, salad specks from lunch on the dental impressions, and a few hairs stuck in the indentation made by his head.

Though grateful he wasn't injured, Ted worried that Titanium White acrylic up his nose and in his mouth might be poisonous. He stripped off his clothes and showered hard.

By the time he scoured the Titanium White from his pores, the acrylic on the canvas had set permanently. There was no question of scraping it off to paint over it.

Ted fumed. The canvas—an investment—might now be worthless. Jamming it back into his car, he drove it to the Saville

Row Gallery downtown to ask the owner, Jack Snell, how to remove acrylic.

Snell saw Ted drive up and thought he still worked for the stock brokerage, which had a busy account at Saville Row—buying art to decorate lobbies and offices, plus their corporate art collection held as an investment and lent to museums for PR.

"Glad to see you!" Snell enthused. "What have we here? Oh! A Pollinski? Mmmm, it's not signed."

"I did this—" Ted began.

"*You* did this!?" Snell stepped back and formed his hands into a telescope to examine the painting without peripheral distraction. "I had no idea you were an artist! Here, here, come inside with this." He gestured Ted into the gallery and cleared wall space to lean the canvas.

Snell shook Ted's hand. "Do you have more? Enough for a one-man? Are they all large and monochromatic?"

Ted held his breath and listened with Little Prince pride. "Just this one, today," he said. "Omigosh, I forgot to sign it!" He grabbed a pen from his pocket and—as he leaned forward—decided "Teddy" was juvenile; "Theo" was how he felt today.

"How original, to sign acrylic with ballpoint ink," Snell said. "It's bold."

Theo blushed and swallowed. "Well, it's fast."

When he arrived home, there was a message on his answering machine: "Theo! Jack Snell here. My partner, Fernande, is doing a show of Emerging Artists next month, and she wants to include you. Could you bring in, say, six more pieces by the fifteenth of next month? Call me."

Theo hopped around his living room, yipping with joy, until a neighbor pounded on the wall.

The pounding focused him in reality. "What will I paint?" he asked himself. "*How* will I paint?" he begged the still-price-tagged brushes on his dining table. He began to sweat and whimper as fear of failure and humiliation dueled a ferocious Teddy, who refused to give up his easel.

Theo heard, with stunning clarity, Teddy's shrill voice: "We are 'Physical Abstractionists' synergizing elements of the physical world in fresh and unexpected ways." Teddy whispered, "Do what works!"

Theo ordered ten more canvases, ranging from nine-foot squares to eleven-foot squares, and pint bottles of his ten favorite colors. By the time the supplies were delivered, he was ready.

Onto a bottle of black paint he fell—in a tuxedo, with poise. He dived onto a bottle of aqua in his bathing suit, leaving chest hairs and an impressive bulge. Bringing himself to a rage, he trampled and clawed a pint of scarlet, scattering matches across the fiery acrylic.

By then, however, his skin itched from soapy showers. So he lured a neighbor's cat in, to roll in a pint of sienna for a whole can of tuna. But bathing the cat was worse than showering, so Theo decided to evolve as an artist.

He tracked mud across a long canvas, titling it "Intermediate Steps." He sprayed it with fixative to hold each glob in place.

He smeared his lunch on another canvas; then drizzled paint across the food to be sure it was art.

Fernande explained the gallery's contract. Theo was thrilled to hear the prices Saville Row assigned his paintings...but the gallery took 50%!!

Theo said nothing to Fernande, but he peed on a huge sheet of watercolor paper and titled it "Dawnscape I" and included it in the Emerging Artists show. When a canvas framer overcharged him for a new load of canvases, he created "Dawnscapes II" through "IV."

Saville Row Gallery's Emerging Artists show was a smash hit, and all of Theo's works but "Dawnscape I" sold to museums and private collectors. Fernande lectured him on "productivity."

Theo paced his condo-studio. He needed new works for shows in New York, Paris, and London. "Dawnscapes" weren't selling. Anyway, he wanted to *avancer* his *garde*.

"Hah!" He stamped the floor.

His neighbor kicked the wall.

"I shall sculpt!" Theo exulted.

He telephoned his old marble-sculpting professor for the names of good models. Each day he hired individuals and pairs to pose for him. When the models hit good poses, he and a technician named Ronnie made casts of them, then plaster figures from the casts. Theo sprayed the plaster figures with resin sealant to protect them from water and scratches.

One of his favorite sculptural groupings was a contemporary

Three Graces spoofing Picasso, alluding to Raphael, reprising a Hellenistic statuary group.

Eventually, Ronnie tired of carrying bulky plaster figures to galleries and developed a hollow-figure molding technique that used sturdy, waterproof resins to make unbreakable, portable statues. Theo abandoned painting altogether and became a full-time sculptor.

Fernande telephoned one morning, lisping with rage. "The early plaster figures are disintegrating! Are you using cheap materials?"

Theo blushed and stammered, thinking as fast as he could. "Are people being rough with them?"

"Only if standing on a pedestal is too strenuous for your sculptures."

"I'll have Ronnie over there in no time, to make it right! Where is this sculpture with a problem?"

Fernande read him eight names and addresses. "I'd do the museums first, galleries second, and private collectors third."

Theo and Ronnie decided to simply recast the plaster figures in the new resin process and give the collectors brand new versions. Lighter and easier to move, sturdier to dust.

Theo's sculpting processes were so quick and efficient that he surpassed Fernande's demands for "product," with time left for travel. He moved into a larger studio with skylights, a dressing room for models, and space for vats of fiberglass and resins. To fill the hours Fernande pressured him to think and create—far more than a genius needed—he chain-smoked and read paperbacks.

Theo *loved* art jokes—like framing a mirror, titling it "Variable Self Portrait," and selling it for $100,000.

He slammed a hatchet into a gallery wall and titled it "Rage."

He hired a mime to stand on a black box and imitate gallery patrons, under the title "Watcher." For other galleries, he hired tap dancers, ballerinas, and Flamenco soloists who'd dance on a box for minimum wage and bring their own music. He named them "Rhythm," "Motion," and "Untitled."

He dumped a case of Legos on the floor, with a sign:

MAKE SOMETHING. LEAVE IT HERE ———→

The title, a tour de force, was "Form and Color in Three Dimensions." The problem was if people liked what they made, or had children, they stole the Legos. Ronnie had to keep restocking.

Next, Theo placed a wastebasket on a pedestal. Viewers responded. "Continuous Change" evolved daily, from wadded Kleenex and shiny gum wrappers to museum ticket stubs and pocket lint. The guards had to empty it early the day someone contributed a disposable diaper. People were grateful, actually, for a place to clean out purses and pockets.

Theo discovered the power of *fame* when he enlarged a newspaper photo of movie queen LaDonna Bellebouche to a six-foot square, glued it on a canvas, and colored her lips red with a crayon. Galleries vied for it. When he made four of them, collectors snapped them up.

"Hey!" he told Ronnie. "Let's do only sexy, famous people who've already done the grindy part: creating a wow persona and making their names household words."

Fernande concurred. "Easy to publicize your LaDonna shows. People feel they're coming to see *her*. Keep it up!"

Theo's biggest collector hung the largest LaDonna over his bed. "What an investment!" Sam Sharpnail raved. "I can collect great art and sleep with LaDonna Bellebouche! Is this America or what?"

Theo pampered his major collectors. He enlarged a news photo of Sam Sharpnail—as huge as LaDonna—and felt-tip-penned his eyes blue. He tucked up Sharpnail's double chin by coloring it black, like a shadow under a virile jaw. But Sharpnail's most distinctive feature was his bushy eyebrows. When Theo glued two strips of brown acrylic fur in place, it was perfect.

In fact, Sharpnail promised his modern art collection to the Municipal Art Gallery and endowed a new wing to hold it—in a contract guaranteeing that his own grand portrait by Theo would hang beside LaDonna Bellebouche's eternally.

Theo felt like Teddy, and never shared his easel.

Theo adored fame; he seduced his public with news photos and sound bites. Bony-thin from chain-smoking and prematurely white-haired from inhaling resin fumes, he photographed dramatically and was a favorite for magazine covers. He counted their subscribers as fans. He swam in tropical seas, danced with beautiful women, weekended with princes. His fame encrusted the globe, spread by galleries and collectors, publicists and Teddy.

One summer evening, in a London television interview, a reporter asked Theo what legacy he hoped to leave his collectors.

"My statues and paintings!"

"I mean," the reporter asked, "What will your oeuvre contribute to art history?"

As Theo blanched, Teddy spoke up. "My art is accessible to Everyman—playful yet grounded in everyday experience. I paint and sculpt for real people. And they buy my work."

The interviewer leaned close in sly confidentiality. "What *ideas* do you communicate—to the millions who see your work in museums? And to those lucky collectors who live with your art?"

"Ideas!!? They're sculptures!"

The interviewer's eyes clouded. His mouth turned down.

Theo went blank. Teddy jumped forward—and laughed. "Just kidding! My art is a private … um, experience … shared by me with art lovers. It's personal—what each of us wants it to be. Yes. And, as a physical representation of ideas, no sculpture can be explained in words."

Back in his studio, Theo rolled the interview over and over in his mind. He made himself gloomy.

For the first time in his art career, Teddy doubted.

Theo closed the studio draperies, curled onto a model's platform, and slept. When he awoke, he smoked a pack of cigarettes; then slept again.

But when he awakened this time, he had the answer: He made statues; art collectors bought them. If collectors bought them, they were art. The interviewer had asked a silly question.

Theo enjoyed sculpting—especially when he found good models with interesting bodies and poses—and especially when Ronnie did the smelly work with the resins. If Theo made a pile of money, then of course people were jealous. He was a genius, and jealousy is a genius' occupational hazard. He took a tropical cruise, to relax.

When he returned, he found a publisher who'd make a coffee table book of his paintings, and another of his sculptures. And glossy calendars in two styles: flip-over and annual date book with a satin ribbon.

Theo grew old—fairly fast, with his chain-smoking and sculpture resining—so he planned his own funeral and monument. He wanted an open casket with double lines of mourners, and a sepulcher based on the Lincoln Memorial. He ordered a likeness of himself seated on a fancier chair than Lincoln's, looking out over a lake for eternity.

He chose the most expensive, elegant mortician to the stars. "For your last show," the mortician said, smoothing his hair, "you want the best, right?"

The additions to the standard contract filled four pages, and the sum was staggering. Theo paid cash.

He hired the most famous tomb-carver in the nation. "Can you handle a job this big?"

"No problem," the monument-maker assured him. "I'll set twenty workers on it, day and night, starting now. Our best quarry. Costs extra, but it's worth it."

Eventually, Theo died.

The undertaker picked up the body from the studio, made a quick plaster cast of the head and glued a life-size photo of Theo's face onto it. He attached the plaster head to a mannequin to fill the coffin and left Theo in the mortuary fridge.

The monument-maker bought a fiberglass model of the Lincoln Memorial and added two finials to Lincoln's chair. Wearing a red plastic apron, he made a fiberglass mask from the mortician's plaster cast of Theo's head and glued it onto the Lincoln statue, sprayed the whole structure with marble dust and liquid glue, then piled rocks in it to keep it from blowing over.

The monument-maker was pleased. "This thing'll last five or ten years, easy," he told his assistant, "unless we get rain."

The Woman
Who Loved
Her Husband

There was once a woman who loved her husband. Myrna loved Stanley so much that she wanted him to be healthy and live forever—or at least as long as she did. Myrna interpreted "The way to a man's heart is through his stomach" as "The way to keep a man's arteries clean is to feed him health food." But Stanley was a big man who liked ice cream.

Before going to her office each morning, Myrna prepared Stanley breakfasts of pasture-raised-chicken eggs or steel-cut oats. She stirred nutritional yeast for B vitamins into pomegranate juice for heart health, and steeped white tea for antioxidants. Stanley ate the health breakfasts, then bought chocolate donuts and Cokes from a vendor at work.

Aproned to protect her professional clothes, Myrna packed health lunches: sandwiches on home-baked bread, peaches she grew in their back yard, and goat cheese from her sister's organic goats. Of course, she used no pesticides and fertilized her trees and garden with goat droppings and compost. Stanley emptied his lunch bucket into a trashcan by the entrance to his office building and ordered Bunches-a-Burgers and a triple Big Thurstee with the other guys at work.

Dinners were wild salmon or trout with brown rice and vegetables from her garden. Stanley ate it all; then disappeared into the basement, to his case of Heath bars, eating enough to even the rows in the box.

At his annual physical, Stanley's cholesterol, blood pressure, and weight were even higher. And Myrna noticed in the sunlight that tiny blood vessels in his nose tip and cheeks had ruptured, and creases across his earlobes were deepening, predicting a heart attack.

She lay awake nights, making sure he was breathing. His snoring, far from reassuring her, reminded her of a stridor's link to sleep apnea.

Myrna took vacation days to double her rows of spinach, cooking onions, and garlic. She planted an avocado tree and aerated her garden's soil.

Pruning, watering, and weeding the new food crops left her no time after work to play her electric keyboard with the automatic rhythm section, and the sleepless nights left her groggy. But Stanley was her crusade. At dinner, she served him the tenderest eggplant slices and perfectly sun-ripened strawberries—eating those with tiny bug holes herself, or going without because she was struggling with nausea, anyway. She waited until they were ready for dessert to pick the boysenberries, so the berries would lose no vitamin C by dozing on the counter during dinner. He ate the organic dinners; he could see how much it meant to her. But he did have time to zip to the basement while she was picking and washing boysenberries.

"Boy, honey," he said one morning, "those brown spots on your cheek … You sure that big one's okay?"

Myrna's dermatologist froze off the spots and biopsied the big one, ordering her to stay out of the sun. Then he referred her to an internist for her strange color and fatigue. The internist discovered that exhaustion had made her vulnerable to a rare virus that was usually rapidly fatal. But something—her mega-nutrition or perhaps a life-mission—was fanning her sputtering vital flame. In a state of near-collapse, she was hospitalized near Stanley's office so he could visit her often.

She begged her sister Sybil to make health food for Stanley so his cholesterol wouldn't skyrocket before she could get back on her feet. Sybil agreed to prepare exactly the lunches and dinners he was accustomed to.

The first days in the hospital, Myrna was hooked to an IV in the Intensive Care Unit. But early one morning, she was gurneyed to a private room in the north wing. As the nurse helped her into bed, Myrna realized that Stanley's office building was directly across a parking lot from her window. At 8:45 A.M., she wobbled to her window to wave to Stanley and surprise him. Looking across the parking lot, to the side entrance and office window, she stood ready.

Oddly, a cluster of animals was assembling beside the building. Stray dogs growled at each other, cats clung to power poles nearby, and sparrows perched on window ledges. At 8:50 a homeless man pushing a well-organized shopping cart sped into the lot and tried to shoo the dogs and cats that circled him, barking and hissing, refusing to leave.

At 8:53 Stanley's car appeared in the lot. Myrna waved, but he evidently didn't see her.

By 8:56 Stanley reached the side entrance to his building. Myrna struggled to open her window to call to him, but the window was sealed shut to protect the air-conditioning.

At 8:57 Stanley opened his lunch bucket, filled by Sybil to Myrna's specifications, and dumped his organic sandwich, peach, hand-squeezed orange juice, hard-boiled pasture-raised egg, and homemade yogurt into the trashcan by the door, then disappeared into the building.

The homeless man kicked savagely at the dogs leaping into the trashcan. The dogs were as strong as dingoes, and the weather-beaten man was amazingly agile. He grabbed the peach and yogurt; one dog snatched the sandwich while another gobbled the egg. The orange juice spilled, and a third dog lapped the sidewalk dry. The sparrows pecked up every crumb of egg and sandwich, and a cat caught one of the sparrows.

Myrna couldn't breathe for a moment. Did Stanley stumble and his lunch bucket latch fail?

There, on the third floor, Stanley's office light came on. Through his large window, she could see him take off his coat and hang it up. He answered his telephone. He gestured to someone and then, a minute later, put something in his mouth. It looked very much like a chocolate donut. He chewed. Then he opened a can of cola and sipped.

She sat on the edge of the bed. An hour later, when the nurse came in with meds, Myrna was still staring out the window, her eyes dry from not blinking. Stanley had eaten three donuts with two cans of soft drinks.

"Lie down!" the nurse said. "You're here to rest and stimulate your immune system." She pressed Myrna into bed and tucked the blankets around her chin. "You're cold!"

There was a different look in Myrna's eyes. The nurse handed her a tiny white paper cup with four pills in it; she swallowed them. But she was battling betrayal instead of her virus.

Did Stanley not love her and want to live as long as she did? Was he discarding *her* with his lunch? Her temples pounded as tears ran into her ears. She vowed to confront Stanley during visiting hours.

Don't you know the value *of organic food?* she would ask him.

Her mind answered for Stanley, *Who is the one in the hospital?*

Yes, she'd parry, *but could you, with your sodas and donuts and whatever you eat for lunch, defeat this deadly virus?*

No answer.

She snuffled. *And I got it by gardening, trying to make you healthy!*

Stanley stood there in her mind. A big man who likes ice cream. Her best friend. With a sense of humor. A very loving man ... except for this. An easygoing guy who ate health dinners and pretended to eat health lunches to please her.

My garden, Myrna decided finally, *is mine. You have a right to your own tastes.* She turned over. *And maybe organic breakfasts and dinners plus junk lunches equals moderation!*

She sighed, exhausted. And that scared her. She had to fight the virus, not Stanley. He was on his own. Just like her.

She closed her eyes and relaxed completely, imagining a powerful pink light bathing her body to strengthen phagocytes and T-cells. She willed the pink light to shrivel the virus attacking her. She breathed diaphragmatically, oxygenating her cells, and flexed the muscles in her legs to circulate the oxygen and newly empowered phagocytes and T-cells.

At lunch, she ate the hospital's deceased carrots and ex-broccoli beside chicken limbs swimming instead of flying, and on her dinner request form, she crossed out dessert and requested double fruit. Then she called Sybil. "Could you bring me the pomegranate juice and yeast during visiting hours instead of making it for Stanley tomorrow morning? I don't think he wants it."

"He doesn't like my cooking," Sybil said. "He's eating Heath bars in the basement."

"Can you bring me a basket of whatever's ripe in my

garden?"

Sybil made her get her doctor's okay.

In two days, Myrna was home.

With the calendar devouring her sick leave, she crawled from bed to her garden to eat the best strawberries, warm from the sun, and peaches so perfect the color was obviously named for them. She set up her steamer, then plucked baby beets and adolescent spinach to steam before they realized what was befalling them. She meditated, drank mineral water, and bathed herself in the amazing pink light that viruses cannot survive. Every day she felt better. Stanley looked no worse, making his own lunches and dinners.

When Myrna went back to cooking dinners for two, she prepared food she wanted them both to eat, but cut the best zucchini in half and shared it. And for dessert, she put the purplest boysenberries in her own bowl.

The day before Myrna returned to work, Stanley hugged her tight. "Thank you for saving my beloved. I know—it was your health foods."

She nodded into his big, warm shoulder.

But when she dusted off her keyboard and started playing *Louis Louis* with the Bossa Nova rhythm accompaniment, he disappeared into the basement.

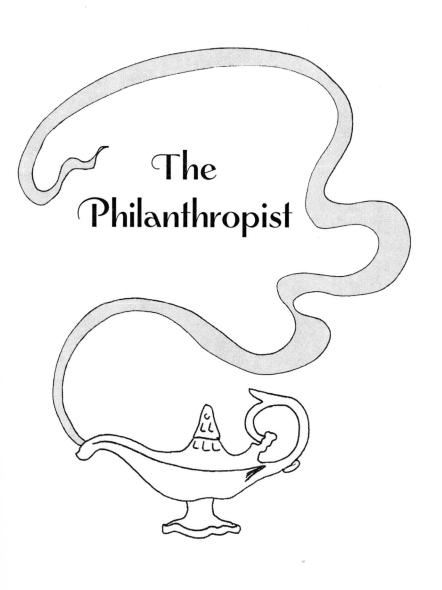

The
Philanthropist

A young man named Roger burned to be rich and famous. He worked in his father's shoe store, and it nearly killed him to kneel before strangers and measure their feet.

"Patience, Roger," said his father. "We influence the nation by fitting shoes in our town. When people's feet hurt, their minds can't function."

Roger didn't argue, but his eyes narrowed.

At lunch he told his father, "Farthington's dozing in the stockroom, again."

"He's thinking. Farthington figures out how to fit children

too young to tell us what hurts—and teenagers who'd grow ten bunions before they'd fight peer pressure. He's committed to making a difference."

Roger's sandwich turned dry in his mouth. Since lunch was already ruined, he brought up Mrs. Schuster, who did their bookkeeping and answered the phone besides selling shoes. "Mrs. Schuster can be replaced by a computer and answering machine."

"She's a young widow and needs this job to support her children. Anyway, her smile sells a hundred pairs a year."

"She can get another job. You're supposed to turn a profit in your store, not find her a job."

"Well, I make a profit. Are we so well fed we have to diet and work out at a gym? Do we drive good cars and live in nice houses? Did you and your sister have braces on your teeth and go to college?"

Roger threw the rest of his sandwich in the wastebasket. "I'll reorganize the sport shoe display," he said in a very smooth voice.

That Christmas, a shipping crate of work boots fell off a truck squarely and fatally onto Roger's father. Roger inherited the store on January first. "How fitting," he mentioned to his rearview mirror while driving to work. His mind swirled with new displays and business hours, and return-for-credit-only policies.

When he arrived to unlock the doors, Mrs. Schuster and Farthington were waiting. "We'll miss your father," Mrs. Schuster said.

"A wise, good man," Farthington added.

"Patience," Roger muttered to himself. The first thing he did inside the store was to arrange a brand new Teen Table with colorful shoes displayed around a tall cactus.

Farthington approached the table. "Those lightweight loafers have no support. They're okay for social events, but we can't encourage those for school."

Roger looked levelly at his employee. "We can encourage whatever they want to *buy*, Farthington. It's a free country."

"But their parents trust us to—" Farthington stopped talking and remembered a customer he'd promised to call when the extra-narrow running shoes came in.

Roger spent the rest of the morning examining employee benefits to see how much Farthington's and Schuster's health insurance and retirement plans cost the company. It was appalling. Farthington, in particular, had worked there so many years that his pay was nearly triple the minimum wage.

At lunchtime, Roger squinted at Schuster and Farthington chatting and laughing over their sandwiches. They reminded him of butcher shop outlines of steers with their cuts of meat labeled. He saw little dotted lines sectioning them into rump roasts and briskets, marked with prices per pound: Overpriced! Extravagant! Too much pot roast; not enough filet mignon! They'd have to work more to be worth their cost to him.

After lunch he told Mrs. Schuster to finish the billing and shelve the new stock before closing time; if she couldn't do just that little bit, she'd have to work late on her own time. He told Farthington to take afternoons off from now on. They needed more efficiency in the shoe store.

For the Easter rush he hired a high school boy for minimum wage and no retirement plan, instead of reinstating Farthington, who took a night job to pay his rent. An explosion at Farthington's night job made him late to the shoe store one morning, so Roger could finally fire him and hire a college girl part-time without benefits, saving enough to remodel the store.

Mrs. Schuster didn't smile so much anymore, selling shoes bought for style, not support, with part-time employees who didn't know lasts from laces. She felt the weight of being an owner (she wasn't) on her shoulders and the emptiness of being an unwanted employee (she was) in her stomach. When Roger stopped the Christmas bonuses and switched her health insurance to a veterinary group, Mrs. Schuster quit.

Roger replaced the cash registers with point-of-sale computers that told how much change to give so he could hire high school dropouts too weak in math to question their paychecks. He computerized all purchasing, inventorying, billing, and sales. He bought a sleek automated attendant telephone system and laid off two part-time college students who were troublemakers. He doubled the workloads of all employees and figured out the longest possible shifts without dinner breaks. With the net savings, he bought the store next to his and opened a clothing boutique. He networked his two stores' computers and hired more part-timers who could be worked hard, paid little, denied benefits, and fired easily.

He called himself "Roger the Barber" because he was a genius at shaving expenses. He bought more buildings and found new ways to shave dimes off costs here and dollars off expenses there, then pad what he charged renters here and lessees there.

He never read books on shoes or feet; he studied *How to Pay No Income Tax!* and *101 Ways to Squeeze More from Employees*. He finally married when he met a woman who'd inherited eighteen million dollars and an obsessive-compulsive personality disorder that didn't allow her to buy anything new. She bought her wedding dress at a garage sale. Then resold it.

Roger enjoyed power. He bought every rundown building near his store and proposed an inner-city reclamation project named Rogerville. He donated tax-deductible funds to re-landscape a park next to his shopping center and a tax-deductible grant to refurbish the old opera house next to his hotel. He relished special bank loans and how fast his calls went through. He hired a timid secretary to watch her flinch when he yelled.

His fortune grew. His investments metastasized into cities and states beyond his own. He put shoe factories in countries where people would work even full-time without health insurance, in unsafe buildings. He dimmed lights and plugged drinking fountains to shave utility bills. He sold customers' private information to telemarketers around the world.

He was happy at last—so rich and powerful that Presidential candidates courted his endorsement at exquisite dinners. (He played hard to get.)

But Roger's hair was graying, his wife was flabby, his children were somewhere. He would not live forever, and he wanted everyone to remember how rich and powerful he was. Roger the Barber was a shrewd man, and the world never has enough shrewd men.

So he became a philanthropist. He looked over his city to see which people he wanted to remember him. He liked rich people, so he donated money for an art museum named Galerie Roger. Secretly hoping to live forever, he funded The Roger Wing at a leading research hospital. He'd never been good at sports—chosen last for teams at school—so he built an enormous gymnasium for his university, forcing athletes to say "Roger Gym" thousands of times a day and sportscasters to broadcast the magic name to sports fans.

One winter afternoon as he strolled past The Roger Opera House, beyond Hotel Roger, along refurbished Rogerville Avenue to Roger Park, he was irritated by idlers sleeping on his park benches and cluttering his park lawns with cardboard houses. "You, there!" he bellowed, pounding on a refrigerator crate lying on its side. "Clean up this mess and move on! Have you no sense of property? No work ethic? Any responsibility? Are you feeding at the public trough, sucking dry the people who work hard for their living?"

Liking the sound of his anger, he let his voice soar into outrage. "Whose work made this lovely park possible? Do you know who I am?"

The refrigerator crate shuddered as someone pushed open its end flaps. It was a woman who'd bent double to fit inside. As she straightened up to squint at Roger through a haze of fatigue, other boxes opened, and grimy cocoons of newspapers and rags stood up from park benches. "We do, indeed," said Mrs. Schuster. "Do you know who *we* are?"

Roger stared at her dull hair and unflattering work uniform. Mrs. Schuster had let herself go! She wasn't smiling, but when she spoke, he could see she was missing some teeth.

Farthington, carrying a lunch pail, walked from a bench to glare into Roger's face. Two women wearing thick eyeglasses and carpal tunnel wrist braces climbed out of cardboard boxes to shake their fists at Roger. Three greasy men carrying wrenches scowled at him. Then too many people to count began circling him, closer and closer, until their shoulders bumped his. A tall man flicked Roger's hat off. One of the greasy men tousled his hair.

Roger pushed to the edge of the crowd, but the tall man grabbed his arm. Children were crying—shrill noises that made his head throb.

A loud whistle blew, and workers finishing their day shift

poured into Roger Park. The crowd, enormous now, was muttering and swarming. Men with callused hands pulled at his clothing and snatched wisps of his hair.

"Get away!" he shouted to a woman grabbing buttons from his suit coat. She laughed and shoved her hands into his pockets.

Circling Roger, the crowd found a chant: "*Who* built this?! *Who* built this?!" Louder and closer to him they chanted, stepping on his shoes, their breath filling his nostrils. "*Who* built this?! *Who* built this?!"

Roger recoiled. His mind, ever alert near opportunity, tripped over itself amid confusion and terror. The despicable closeness of unworthy people made his heart pound in his ears.

"Get back!" he shouted. "I'll call the police!"

But the crowd chanting "*Who* built this?" stripped his suit coat from him to find his miniature telephone and computer, pulled his trouser pockets inside out and shared his wallet and keys.

In the distance, he could see the windows of his buildings come alive as hotels and offices, stores and restaurants filled with workers entering his palaces to see what their work had built.

Two men climbed the façade of the Hotel Roger. With work-hardened hands and powerful arms, they twisted the R, O, G, E, and R from the marble and threw them in the street. A woman in a cleaning lady's uniform pulled a pen from her purse and neatly printed her name on the hotel wall. A heavily muscled man in stone-dusty clothes grabbed a fallen R and, with a sharp end, carved his name beside the hotel entrance. Glass shattered and smoke matured into flames. Sirens swooned into the mob.

Roger found his trampled coat and shook the dust from it. He stuffed his pockets back inside his trousers and bent over to retie his shoes. There on the sidewalk was a penny. He picked it up and slid it into his pocket. His eyes narrowed as he scanned the clutter of cardboard houses in his park. *Where do they buy food?* He pictured a chain of Rogerburger Restaurants selling thick buns, thin meat, and days-old lettuce.

But his hands were trembling and when he smoothed his hair into place, one hand came back bloody. Outrage! Someone had pierced his skin! His left eye felt prickly and hot.

He tucked his shirt into his trousers and put his coat on. He stood tall, exhaling dignity to spare. The unruly peasants would pay for this.

A lance of white-hot pain struck his chest, dropping him to his hands and knees. Nausea washed up his torso. Sweat stung his face. He could barely breathe. "Heart attack!" he gasped. He looked to the skyline—across his park and four blocks up a hill to the Roger Wing of Municipal Hospital. He had funded cardiac research; now it would save him.

He staggered to a taxi at the edge of Roger Park. "Municipal Hospital! Immediately!"

The cabbie scanned Roger with a professional eye, from bloody crown and swollen eye, past wrinkled shirt and filthy expensive suit, to scuffed shoes. "Where's your money?"

Roger grabbed for his wallet, patted his pockets. Nothing but the penny. The mob had taken even his handkerchief. "I'm *Roger!*" he said. "This is my Park!" He swung his arm in an arc behind him. The cabbie smirked.

"That's my Hotel and Opera House, and this is my Street and—"

"Right, buddy. Don't scare my customers."

A woman wearing a suit stepped into the taxi, and the cabbie drove away.

A giant pincer clamped Roger's chest. Pain squeezed tears from his eyes, and terror pushed him toward the hospital on foot. Pulling himself forward on trees and lampposts, he struggled past Roger Opera House, closed for the season, and Roger Bank, closed for the day. Clutching at his bank's windows for support, he didn't recognize his reflection. White hair stuck out in bloody wisps; his left eye was swelling and purpling, contorting his face. Dirt smudged his cheeks and torn coat.

Onward he struggled, step by step to the Roger Wing for help. "First class emergency room," he wheezed. "VIPs go straight to the top."

At last he grabbed the brass handle of the Roger Wing Emergency Entrance door. The pain in his chest barely let him sneak inhales and exhales. He aimed himself at the massive admitting desk, a semicircle of glossy wood and marble around a lovely admitting nurse.

"Heart attack!" he gasped to her. "Help, quick, I'm Roger."

She asked for his insurance card.

"My wallet was stolen this afternoon. But I'm Roger. I built this wing."

"Do you have insurance? How will you be paying for this?"

"Searing pain, crushing chest," he whispered. "Cardiac Unit. Quick."

She cleared her throat. "If you're not insured, you'll have to pay before service, sir. Have a seat here in the waiting room. Someone will be with you shortly."

"I'm *Roger!*"

"And I'm Carlita. Now take a seat in the lobby; we'll call you when someone can help you."

He stood his ground. "Do you see who I am?"

Carlita looked.

"This is an Armani suit. And a Rolex 'President' watch—was here." He slid his sleeve up his naked arm. "My *portrait* on the wall!" He stood under it, wheezing. "I financed Dr. Sneff's cardiac research. Get him here *immediately!* I'm *ill!*"

Carlita let her irritation show. "We had a riot out here this afternoon, sir, and we're swamped. You'll have to take a *seat!*"

He pounded the desk. It didn't echo.

Carlita picked up the telephone. "Security? We have a man demanding to see Dr. Sneff. Delirious and violent. We need to get him out of here. Code Green."

When two security guards hustled Roger out of the hospital, he kicked one of them in the groin. They wrestled him to the sidewalk and stomped his ankles against the pavement.

One guard put his foot on Roger's chest.

"I'm Roger! This's my Wing! Call Sneff this instant!"

The guards settling their feet on his chest and ankles called the police on their cell phone. "Hope I don't get senile when *I* get old," one said.

"Or do we have a little drinking problem?" asked the other.

Roger felt the weight on his chest grow heavier than a safe. He couldn't tell if the guard's shoe or his own heart was pressing the life out of him. "Help me!" he called, or perhaps he only wanted to say it.

Anyway, the guards were laughing and sharing a candy bar as Roger stopped yelling and struggling and breathing.

Mrs. Schuster, walking past the Roger Wing, saw the guards nearly standing on a man.

Shifting her grocery bag from one hand to the other, she marched up the steps. "Young man," she faced each of the guards in turn, "would *you* want to be treated like this, even if you were penniless and powerless?" She shooed their feet off the dying man with the authority of competence and bent over to help the poor dirty fellow.

One of the guards checked Roger's pulse. "Uh-oh."

Mrs. Schuster noticed something familiar about the man's eyes, even closed. And his nose and ears. She remembered his suit from the riot in the park. "Roger," she whispered. She picked up his hand and patted it gently. "Oh, Roger. We'll take you inside. I'll tell them who you are."

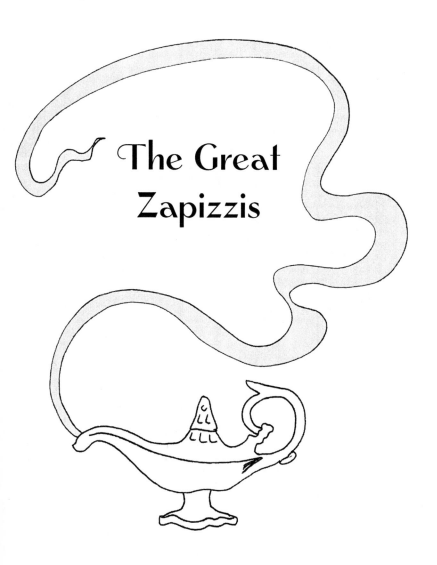

The Great
Zapizzis

The Great Zapizzis were trapeze artists world-famous for their daring tricks, flashy style, and exotic costumes. They performed in the world's finest circus and sometimes on television.

One morning when Luigi Zapizzi was eight years old, his father took him to the main tent for a frank talk. "My dear son," Papa said, "when you were a baby, sweet Mama—between hugs and kisses—dangled you from her thumbs; and I swung you gently by your heels. We taught you simple Zapizzi routines. Now," he paused to smile, "would you like to learn daring ones and join The Great Zapizzis under the big top?"

Papa's confident voice comforted Luigi. Evenly muscled and completely focused, Papa Zapizzi had flawless timing and no fear. He was one of the greatest "catchers" of all time, and other aerialists trusted him with their lives. But Luigi stopped breathing for a minute when his father said "join the Great Zapizzis under the big top."

Papa curled his warm, strong arm around Luigi's shoulders. "You are—even among Zapizzis—special on the trapeze."

Luigi nodded. He already knew.

"I want to show you something." Papa unlocked a heavy trunk and took out an ebony box inlaid with ivory. Inside the box lay a green velvet cushion pavéed with emeralds.

"Wow," Luigi whispered.

Papa's voice was serious. "A cushion like this—when you know how to use it—makes life easier." He held the cushion to his own chest and stood tall. Green light reflecting from the emeralds made his khaki tights and tunic look gold. "Emeralds are strongest when they are many, all together, but if you need something *important*—new trapeze, new costume, a tooth fixed—you take out one, two, three, seven emeralds to buy it. Replace them as soon as you can, so when you need them, they're there. Peace of mind. A magic cushion lets you relax and focus on your trapeze."

Handing the cushion to Luigi, Papa kissed him on the head. "Want to try it on a Great Zapizzi Thunder Roll?"

Luigi shivered and nodded.

Papa centered the velvet cushion in the safety net beneath

the trapezes and stepped back. "Try a Thunder Roll on the low trapeze. If you fall, drop onto this cushion—it'll bounce you up to try again. Do a single, first."

Luigi climbed to the trapeze and rosined his hands. A Thunder Roll was difficult; he was proud that his father wanted to see him do one. But he couldn't concentrate 100%, and fell. He aimed for the emerald cushion—and it bounced him right back up to the trapeze. He tried another Thunder Roll, and again he fell. Once more, the cushion snapped him up to the trapeze. He was amazed.

Papa nodded. "Natural talent plus your own style, Luigi. And now a cushion. But, for sure—listen to me—keep the safety net strong, to hold your cushion."

Trapeze work enchanted Luigi. He studied the routines of his father, mother, uncles, aunts, and cousins, and learned extra tricks by reading books and watching other troupes.

Every day in practices, Papa coached and bellowed. "Watch the trapeze—where it is right now—not where you *want* it—or where it was *yesterday!*"

He'd whisper to Luigi, "Put your best gifts to their best use: life's harder if you walk on your hands and eat with your feet."

Or, "Daredevil Doubles are your passion? Do them in matinees to get ready for big shows at night. We become *Great* Zapizzis when we do our *favorite* tricks."

He'd bellow to the troupe, "Expect to be good at what you do! Stay polite, but know you're good. Zapizzis have dash and panache!"

One afternoon Papa growled to Luigi, "Watch Uncle Gorgonio. No need to fall off a trapeze yourself, when you can watch what happens to a man who eats half a ham and drinks four bottles of wine." Rolling Gorgonio out of the safety net, Papa muttered, "His gift to my children is his foolishness." He sadly peeled Gorgonio's photo from the circus poster for the big show that night.

One quiet evening Papa said, "Look outside to reality and listen inside for timing. Your body won't lie to you."

Sometimes he wouldn't bellow. Just smile.

Luigi rebelled. He fell in love with the equestrians' daughter and quit trapezes to stand up on horses. His exquisite balance made it easy. He missed trapeze tricks, though, and dreamed at night of flying.

Returning to trapezes, he was stiff and his timing was off, so he had to be careful. But he understood equestrians and no longer feared horses. When he regained his rhythm, strength, timing, and grace, he was better than ever.

He practiced nine hours a day to join the Great Zapizzis in evening shows under the big top. He developed his own routine and became a star—painted ten feet tall on circus billboards, interviewed on television, and followed by beautiful women.

Papa Zapizzi hurt his shoulder and had to stop performing. He coached full-time and designed new routines. "Legs straight, Luigi!" he'd yell during rehearsals. "Head up, Lorenza. Smile!" And always, before a performance, his Zapizzi Bear Hug and "Check the safety net, Luigi."

Luigi pulled at it, to satisfy his father; but the net belonged to the whole circus, not to The Great Zapizzis, and he didn't know what he was checking for. Holes? It was a *net*! Tight knots? The right position? He checked the net whenever Papa yelled.

He never forgot his emerald cushion, though. He cleaned it often, added stuffing, and stored it in the ebony case. Before each performance, he centered it in the safety net, and whenever he fell, the cushion boosted him right back to the trapeze. Audiences roared amazement.

One Fourth of July, however, before a huge crowd, during one of the Greatest of Zapizzi routines, Luigi's hand slipped from the trapeze. Falling toward his cushion, he smiled and tracked the trapeze to grab it again as soon as the cushion bounced him up.

But when he hit his cushion, one fiber of the safety net popped. Thrupp. Thruppuppupp, three more ripped. Then, thrrrrrrripp, a series of cordlets raveled and the net yawned, dumping him to the floor of the big top.

Luigi wasn't injured because he landed on his cushion. But without a safety net, the trapeze act had to be canceled.

Only Papa worried. Everyone else said, "We'll just buy a

new one, even if it's expensive and takes time."

However, the Zapizzis couldn't find a company making aerialist safety nets anymore. Old craftsmen who handmade them had died, and hammock factories wouldn't retool for one circus net.

So The Great Zapizzis had to disband. Papa retired with Mama to California. Lorenza married Arnulfo the Lion Tamer, and they created a new act; Uncle Sebastiano moved into circus administration.

Luigi took his emerald cushion, flattened by the fall, into the world outside the circus. Carefully, he removed seven large emeralds to pay college tuition. Then three more for law school. He became a dashing trial lawyer, and each year he bought a glittering new emerald for his cushion.

Wherever he went, with his cushion case tucked under his arm, people noticed his confident stride, energy, and adaptability. "He looks you right in the eye," they'd say. "Poised. Trained as an aerialist, you know."

"He's a Zapizzi," others added.

Luigi married a librarian named Sophia, and they had twin daughters, Nicola and Giovanna. Luigi and Sophia—between hugging and kissing their children—dangled them from their thumbs, swung them gently by their heels, and taught them to read thick books. And for the twins' eighth birthday, Luigi and Sophia made two emerald cushions and showed each child how to use her magic cushion to help her very best efforts be excellent.

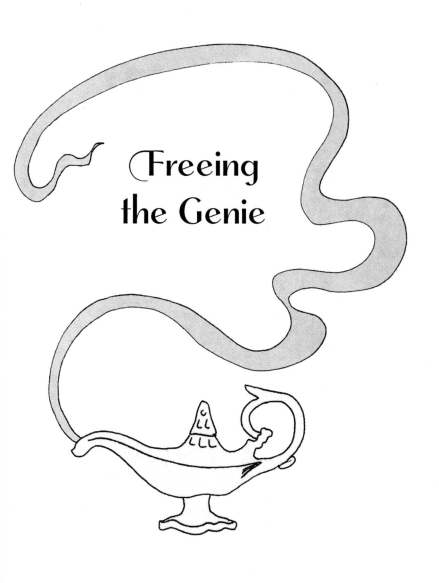

Freeing
the Genie

A woman named Nina knew exactly what she wanted. In an antique shop to buy herself a birthday present—something exotic, she'd know it when she saw it—she found an ancient bronze oil lamp. It was covered with dust, but its elaborate handle and thick spout looked important, its ideal proportions the work of a master artist. So she scooped the lamp from the shelf and talked the shopkeeper into selling it for fifty dollars instead of seventy-five.

At home with a magnifying glass, she searched the lamp for hallmarks to see when and where it was made, and found one tiny cuneiform. The lamp's base was crafted with the same care as its spout, as though for the joy of creating, for the light it would give.

But it was grimy. So, though she respected patinas, she gentled it into warm water.

It trembled in her hands.

She stepped back.

It was silent.

She toweled it dry.

Fumes and vapor bubbled from the spout.

She shrieked and grabbed her fire extinguisher.

The fumes and vapor grew into an exquisite genie wearing little more than an emerald turban. He bathed her in a smile; dark eyelashes swept air when he blinked. He'd been sculpted by the Michelangelo of genies, and his gentle eyes emitted light instead of reflecting it. He bowed graciously from the spout. "For finding me in this curséd lamp, I grant you three wishes!" He swelled and swayed above the lamp. "They must be personal—for *you alone*."

His lovely manners and kind voice softened her fears. And she had wishes! Silently, she prioritized. *This physically stunning creature will understand.* "I wish to have perfect health. Please."

He looked at her. "But you seem—"

"Oh, I'm fine. I work out every day and eat organic food, but health is ..."

The genie nodded. *Whooouufffff!* A great wind roared from the lamp and swirled around her body.

When it quieted, she felt racehorse-sleek, and energy filled her mind and muscles. "Thank you!" she said.

He bowed beneficently. "And your second wish?"

"I want to be my boss's boss. Reorganizing our division at Battedyne could save the company and 500 jobs!"

The genie smiled. *Whooouufffff!* A great wind filled the room, rattling the windows.

The telephone rang.

"Shall I get that?"

He nodded.

It was the CEO of Battedyne. "Nina—Scott Hylund here. Good news! Jim Barnes is taking a job with the government and I want you to replace him. Phil simply can't run your division, so I'm promoting you above him. Can you come in Monday prepared to be Division Chief?"

I'll be my boss's boss! The genie must *be magic.* "Of course," she said.

Scott paused. "Did Jim tell you he was planning to leave?"

"No. But I've been seeing ways to make us more effective. I'll bring my notes in Monday. I'm grateful for this chance."

She said goodbye to Scott and returned to the genie. "Thank you again! I'm my boss's boss!"

The genie straightened his turban. "Have you a third?"

Nina blushed. The genie's long-lashed eyes and rippling muscles awakened her third wish, but wariness stopped her tongue. "May I wait until tomorrow?"

He bowed. "Just rub the lamp." With a gentle hiss, he

shrank back through the spout, and she set the lamp on the dining room table.

She exercised and cooked an organic dinner, trying to think of a different wish. But she knew exactly what she wanted: health, fulfillment, and … It was too important to change.

The next day she bought four new suits, shoes, and a sleeker briefcase, and got a haircut. After running on the beach and stretching, she ate dinner while organizing her notebook of ideas for refocusing her division.

The magic lamp hummed on the table.

She buffed it with a tea towel.

The lamp rocked and hissed as the genie swelled from its spout. "Yesssssssss?"

"Would you like to see—?"

"I would like very much to see the notes and suits. Your hair is beautiful."

She showed him the briefcase and modeled her suits, then explained how each idea would empower her company in a competitive market.

He listened intently.

Each day, Nina felt more at home in slender power suits and a corner office. Some of her ideas worked better than others, but coworkers at Battedyne found they could rely on her for honest, creative thinking.

Every evening after work and working out, Nina freed

the genie to tell him her adventures. He floated above the lamp, smiling at her successes, wincing at disasters, asking questions until he understood.

She read him novels after dinner, twenty pages a night. He loved it. She played the piano and they sang duets.

One Tuesday night, Nina stopped reading *Moby Dick* mid-page and said, "You're magic, of course?"

He nodded. "The real thing, not sleight of hand. Genies work with talent, charisma, creativity, love." He leaned closer. "Genies search for people like you."

She lost her place in *Moby Dick*.

There was a long silence.

"Your third wish, Nina?"

She looked at the genie's glittering eyes, dear smile, powerful torso, and smooth skin—and the genie blushed.

"But granting my third wish," she whispered, "will set you free."

The silence expanded.

She closed her book and looked at the genie. "I wish … to find my own true love."

The genie swelled taller, and there was a great cloud of steam in all colors known on earth plus some not yet encountered. When the steam cleared, the lamp was empty.

She polished the lamp and put it in the center of her mantel.

A week later at Battedyne, the president of a new company, Tekktronixx International, arrived for an appointment with Nina. His tie was emerald silk and his dark eyelashes swept air when he blinked. He was so exquisitely sculpted that Nina's secretary overturned her coffee cup.

The secretary ushered him into the office, and Nina stood up but hung onto her desk. When she reached forward to shake hands, he lifted her hand to his heart.

Her secretary backed out and closed the door.

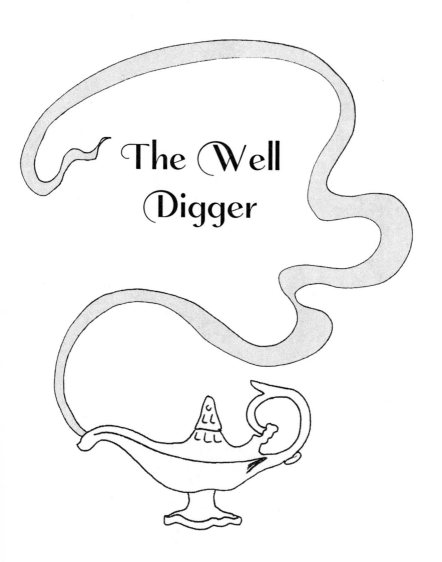

The Well
Digger

A farmer hired a young man to dig a well thirty feet
deep, for fresh, cool water.

On Monday, the well digger brought his pick
and shovel and began digging. But the soil had more stones
than dirt, and he was soon sweaty and cross.

On Tuesday, the well digger brought his brother to help,
but the two argued about the best way to lift stones.

Wednesday was so hot that the well digger rested in the
shade.

On Thursday, a rainstorm softened the hard ground to
mud. The rocks came out easily, but they were slippery.

On Friday, the well digger brought a magician to burn incense and chant the stones to the surface.

On Saturday, the well digger sharpened his shovel as thirsty cows circled him, mooing.

Sunday was the well digger's day of rest.

On Monday, he asked the farmer to pay him for a week's work.

The farmer carried his yardstick to the mud-hole where he wanted a well. "Twenty-one inches," he said. "It's thirty feet to the water!"

"Your land is stony," the young man countered.

"A hole isn't a well until it hits water," the farmer said.

The well digger leaned on his shovel and mopped his brow. "Look how sweaty I am."

The farmer patted the young man on the shoulder and smiled. "We measure a hole by its depth, not by the sweat of the digger. I'll come back this afternoon to measure again." And he left to finish hitching his horse to the plow.

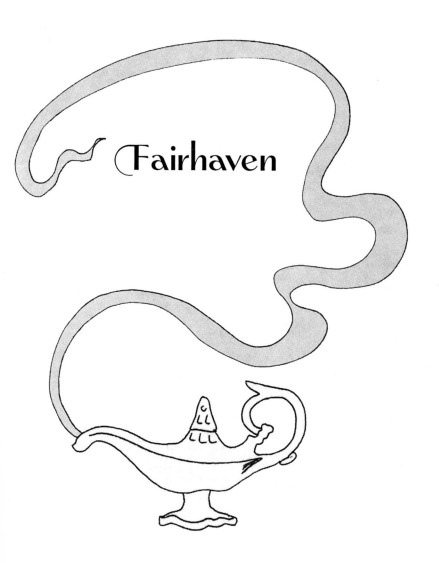

Fairhaven

A farmer named Theon Dormer stayed up late to finish reading a book titled *Absolutely Fair!* At midnight, he read the conclusion on page 312: "Every living thing senses fairness. Each plant and animal in a just environment grows bigger and reproduces faster; any animal or plant treated unfairly weakens and dies."

Theon groaned and slid the book onto his nightstand, guilt saturating him for every cow that dried up early and for the brown patch in his alfalfa field. He writhed at his insensitivity—farming as his father had, as his neighbors did, as though there were no alternative.

After a night of twisted sheets and kicked-off blankets, Theon called his animals to the tidy barnyard bordered by a large red barn and fat silos. He held one hand aloft until the animals quieted. "Friends," he began, "I thank you each for our joy and prosperity on this, the most productive farm in the county." He wiped his sleeve across his eyes. "But I have read a book that will change our lives—*Absolutely Fair!*" He raised the book to show them.

Grazers sighed and dipped for clumps of grass. The cat mimed listening while aligning herself with the sun's rays. Hens rolled their eyes, but hushed their chicks and sat on the wildest ones.

"According to this," Theon continued, "we will all be our healthiest and most productive if we live in absolute fairness." He hugged the book to his chest. "We start today. I'll change the Dormer Family Farm's name to Fairhaven and make a weather vane from a balance scale. Are there any questions?"

A chestnut workhorse named Belle shook her mane. "What hasn't been fair?"

"Little things," Theon said. "I gave the best stalls ... I criticized ... oh, let's ... just begin afresh today—make Fairhaven a sanctuary of perfect equality." He beamed in benevolence and warmth.

The cat walked forward to rub against his overalled leg.

Theon reached down to scratch behind her ear, then jerked his hand away when he realized how long it would take to scratch equally the three hundred ears on his farm.

The cat meowed upward.

"I haven't milk for everyone, Felicity," Theon said. "I can give you some for dinner when we all eat."

That afternoon at the dust baths, one hen mused to another, "To my knowledge, no hen on this farm has ever pulled a cart. We're just expected to lay eggs. Not that eggs aren't important, but we're ... you know ... "

"Taken for granted," said her friend. "It's *assumed* we'll lay eggs."

"Worse for *us!*" said a rooster. "Audition to avoid the oven. It's crow for your life, strut for survival. How do horses feel—knowing they'll pull a few carts, jounce some riders, spend their life in tall grass or getting curried in a stable? *That's* unfairness in *my* book: compare chickens and horses!" He spat a gravel grit.

The chickens felt blood pulsing behind their eyes and swelling their combs.

"Unfairness causes stress, and everyone knows stress kills."

"Theon's making sense this time."

"*Absolutely Fair!* is a great book."

They began sketching fairness demands in the sand, keeping chicks from running through them, considering carefully the equality they wanted to gain.

In the pasture, a middle-aged cow named Lorraine draped her steaming udder against a water trough and spoke earnestly to her herd-mates. "Do you dream of *glamour*—reclining on a couch or Theon's lap and having your ears scratched? A rhinestone collar instead of stainless steel ear tags?"

Her friend Alma nodded. "Our lives are our work—sterile and impersonal." She switched her tail. "Then that *cat* simpers around our milk pumps. Does Ms. Feline care how much alfalfa we have to chew to make an extra bowl of milk? And whom does she thank? *Theon!!!"*

A heifer stepped into the conversation. "Why do you make so *much* milk? When Felicity has kittens, she feeds her six and that's it. Horses the same. Feed their own young, period." Self-confidence and sunlight reflected from her smooth coat.

Felicity the cat, crouching rock-still in the pasture to observe a field mouse, overheard the cows. Barely breathing until they left the meadow, she had plenty of time to think.

An apple tree grunted to his row-mates. "Are apples heavier than other fruit? We carry these blasted things until autumn! Limbs out straight, limbs up tall!"

"Tell me about it! Almond trees don't know the *word* bursitis."

"*Cherry* trees are the whiners. We're *all* ornamental, technically. If you produce flowers, you're ornamental."

"Absolutely. Try spring without apple blossoms."

The first tree sighed and dropped an unripe apple to the ground. It was no accident.

In the horse barn, Belle raised her head from the manger to speak to her colleague in the next stall. "How do you think others see us?"

"As dumb beasts," Star said. "All back, no brains."

Belle snorted. "If they only knew the skill required to pull with a partner a load too heavy for one —"

Star nodded. "—*feeling* in your harness which way to lean, when to speed up, how hard to pull."

"The safety regulations."

"Versatility," Star said. "Who else on this farm switches from plows to carts to wagons to sleighs to carriages in parades, with gewgaws in their mane?"

"Poise. Self discipline. *That's intelligence!*" Belle shook a forelock away from her eyes.

Star leaned her chin on the stall partition. "When you're plowing at dawn, the mist filling the valleys, and you're lunging forward in a satisfying rhythm, do you ever write poetry in your head?"

Belle looked surprised. "No. I write songs."

"I thought I recognized that inward look. Thinking too hard just for plowing."

"You write poetry, then?" Belle asked.

Star shuffled a white-stockinged hoof in the straw. "No one else knows."

"What would it mean to you," Belle asked, "if we wrote it down—your poetry and my songs? If we performed them?"

Star threw back her head and whinnied.

The next morning when Theon awoke, the sun was fading his bedspread and the grandfather clock had run down and stopped. But no cows were mooing to be milked. Silence filled the barnyard; fear squeezed Theon's lungs.

Yanking his overalls on, he ran outside barefoot—and saw at once that he was an unnecessary man.

The cows had nudged open the pens to their calves and were feeding them. Theon watched with alarm the slackening udders and eager calves.

Hens and the rooster had harnessed themselves with string to the hay wagon and were trying to pull it. The rooster strained against his homemade harness until his comb throbbed. A hen lay on her side, panting, an ominous bulge lifting feathers over her breast muscles.

The horses, out of their stalls but not in the pasture, were alternately smoothing the barnyard with their tails and hoofing symbols in the dirt.

Theon looked away, patting his overalls to ground himself. But there in his apple orchard stood naked trees surrounded by puddles of stunty, green apples no good even for hog feed.

"*What,*" screamed Theon, "are you *doing?*"

"We're growing cherries," said the first apple tree.

"And almonds," said the second.

"So we purged the apples," said the third.

Theon whirled to face a rhythmic snorting coming from the pigpen. At their food trough, four pigs grunted softly to each other, sorting their food into two piles. "Bad for us ... healthful ... bad, bad ... healthful." An enormous boar tusked a trench in the ground and a graceful sow named Clio snouted corn and oiled bread into it.

As Theon strode forward, Clio flung last night's leftover spaghetti into the trench. "Why?" Theon asked, trying to keep his voice calm.

The sow never missed a stroke, snouting trenchward the foods sorted by her coworkers into the "bad" category. "If we're ever to be leaders ... as pigs are by natural intelligence ... we must respect our bodies ... We've begun with diet ... Please respect, from now on ... our needs. Exercises ... begin at eleven."

Following her glance with his own, Theon saw a young boar and sow filling seed bags with rocks, weighing them on the fruit scale, and placing a pair of the weights by each of eight carefully shaped exercise wallows.

Theon covered his eyes with his hands. When something stepped onto his bare feet and leaned against his leg, he jumped.

It was Felicity. "Thank you!" She scampered into the barn and melted into its darkness.

"For what?" Theon asked himself because everyone else was too busy to answer. He walked into the house to find his shoes, a shirt, and some breakfast.

Felicity purred to the cows feeding their calves. "Aren't you starved for entertainment? Work is noble, but in excess it dulls the spirit. We all deserve some glitter and music."

"Just yesterday I was telling my friends how I crave glamour!" said Lorraine, the cow Felicity had overheard.

The smooth-coated heifer chewed her cud, remembering the cows' resentment of the cat's luxury supported by bovine exploitation.

Alma leaned down to the cat. "How can we get to town for music and glitter?"

Felicity ignored the hot alfalfa breath. "We deserve our *own* night life. Right here at Fairhaven. Come to the barn at midnight; bring a bowl of cream. You'll have the glamour you deserve."

Felicity walked to the edge of the horses' hoofings. "I had no idea you were artists!" She concentrated on the symbols written in the dirt. "Can you interpret these for me?"

Belle began singing—reading from the earth—songs revering their valley and hills and her intelligent workmate, celebrating equine joys.

When she finished, Star whinnied appreciation as the cat purred praise. Then Star stepped forward to read her lyrical poems

expressing—far more eloquently than the cat had antici-
pated—emotions of animals pawing raw earth they're no longer attuned to because they serve human beings whose feet
don't touch it.

"Ahhhhh," said the cat when Star finished a particularly
moving paean to the thrills and dangers of slippery streets in
heavy traffic. "How many poems have you completed?"

"Just four," said the horse-poet.

Felicity turned to the songsmith. "And how many
compositions?"

"Five," answered Belle.

"Would you two value having your work heard? If I can
provide an audience, will you perform?"

Both horses blushed and whickered.

"That's a yes?" The cat smiled. "Come to the barn just
before midnight, with your songs and poems memorized; I'll
assemble an audience."

Felicity strolled to the pigpen and saw the trench full of
leftover spaghetti, oiled bread, and molding cheese.

"Would you consider selling that?"

The boar stopped kicking dirt onto the spaghetti. "Well,
it's delicious," he said. "A shame to waste. Who's buying?"

"I can arrange a trade," the cat said. "I'm opening a nightclub with original music and cultural entertainment—just
the thing for intellectuals and leaders. I can let you in with no
admission fee if you bring your unwanted foods into the barn
this afternoon. The show starts at midnight."

"Bartering is clever," the boar said. He looked around. The sows nodded.

All eight pigs formed a crew, transporting their unwanted food to the barn. The boar grinned to the graceful sow. "It saves me the time and effort of digging that trench."

Clio smiled back. "Removing temptation's a proven diet technique."

But there were never more than five pigs visible at any time. Snorting and toting, the pigs trotted great mouthfuls of unwanted foods to the barn, grunting "There!" and "Good riddance!" as they dropped the rejects onto straw provided by Felicity.

One by one, though, the pigs carrying food stepped behind their sty for a moment or stopped by a fence to scratch an itch, then returned for another mouthful of food. When the trench was empty and all the food delivered, the cat noticed that no spaghetti and very little oiled bread had made it to the barn. But she said nothing.

Felicity strolled to the apple trees and leaned against the trunk of the tallest, purring sympathetically. "Redefining oneself is sooooo challenging." She rolled onto her back, then winced away from the hard apples. "Especially with all these reminders." She shivered. "Shall I make these disappear for you?"

The apple trees brushed their branches together, thinking.

"You're building new skills and habits," she purred. "These apples are habit-traps. Let me help."

The trees bowed and smiled. "How kind. Please take them. A classic fruit, but we refuse to be exploited."

"Oh, I understand. We're each responsible for our destiny." She scooped the apples into a pile. "By the way, I'm opening a nightclub in the barn. The fun starts at midnight, and I'll leave the barn doors open so you can enjoy the music and poetry." She scampered toward the barn, calling over her shoulder, "Be right back with a bag!"

While Felicity loaded the green apples into a feed sack, the pigs grunted and sweltered in their exercise class. They had designed calisthenics specifically for porcine fitness—side swivels for midriff trimming and flexibility, and long slow stretches to "lengthen the look of those necks and legs."

Dragging apples to the barn, Felicity noticed the rooster pulling a toy fire engine in a circle and crowing. She sat at the edge of the circle. "If you had a costume, this would make a nightclub act."

The rooster stopped in front of her, but not too close. "Thank you."

"I'm opening a nightclub tonight. Looking for acts. Interested?"

The rooster pretended to consider. "It would help all chickens if I appeared in our new role—animals of physical strength—especially rescuers. Count me in. What time?"

"Midnight."

He blinked.

"Until this gets rolling," Felicity said, "I'll have to pay you in food. And, of course, appreciation and applause."

He nodded.

"Midnight in the barn." Felicity started to leave, then turned back and whispered, "What's wrong with your friend?"

Through clenched beak he said, "Abigail is the bravest ... She harnessed herself to Theon's hay wagon and was pulling her mightiest—on the verge of getting it to move—when something popped. We've been giving her sips of water and fanning her."

Felicity stared at the white hen lying in the dust, breathing raggedly, a string harness tangled beside her. "She needs medical attention. She's in pain!"

"But how?" the rooster asked.

"I can take care of her."

"Oh, could you? We're embarrassed to ask Theon—"

"Absolutely," Felicity nodded. "We must solve this ourselves." She walked with the rooster to Abigail, picked her up by the neck, and began dragging her toward the meadow.

Hens ran up, scrawking.

The rooster calmed them.

Through Abigail's feathers, Felicity said, "This is how I carry my own kittens. Abigail will be better soon. I'll keep you informed." She looked at the rooster. "Invite all your friends." She trotted smoothly toward the meadow, Abigail barely flopping between her paws.

At dusk Felicity returned to the courtyard, looking pleased. The chickens rushed her. "How is Abigail?" "What did she injure?"

The cat's voice was soothing. "Abigail's resting much more comfortably now. She has some torn ligaments—which, of course, take a very long time to heal." Genuine concern lit her eyes. "See you at midnight!"

The cows helped Felicity close the barn doors to prepare for the grand opening. Most animals tried to nap to be awake for the nightclub, but their excitement plus mysterious noises coming from the barn made it difficult.

When the moon rose above the apple orchard and Theon turned out his lights, the barn doors swung open—pushed in unison by the horses, clattering their hooves to make a drum roll. Fireflies buzzed in overturned jelly jars from Theon's basement. A shaving mirror dragged from Theon's bedroom reflected the fireflies and moonlight. The barn floor was clawed clean, and green apples were piled in pyramids beside the pigs' corn mounds arranged in clean straw nests. A hundred animals crowded in.

Felicity opened the show by introducing the rooster. In a costume made from bottle caps and a red wool sock, he dedicated his performance to Abigail—too badly injured to attend this evening—wounded in the very struggle to prove that chickens can pull as heavy loads as other animals.

Applause, applause. "Fairness for all!" The animals

stamped and snorted, whinnied and clucked.

Star read her poetry to heartfelt acclaim.

Belle sang three fine songs—one soulful, one romantic, one rousing.

Between acts, Felicity took food orders, mentioning the specialties of the evening. Corn mounds the pigs had rejected as too starchy were perfect for chickens and horses. In the night-club ambiance, though, several pigs did order corn mounds. Green apples were touted as delicacies popular on the coast: tiny servings, crisp, promoting active digestion—mouth-burners and tooth-chippers, but trendy.

There was dancing, conversation, excitement. Night-life! Each animal savored something while giving what others savored. The cows brought extra cream; Felicity was ecstatic.

As the fireflies sank in the jelly jars and the moon rested in the apple trees, Felicity strode to center stage and began singing. Louder and louder, she celebrated fairness for all and opportunity for each. Each yowl was longer, each squeal of joy higher than the one before.

As the most impressive notes extolling the grandest idealism rolled from the cat's throat, Theon, in his pajamas, peeked through a barn window. All his animals were watching Felicity's riveting performance. *Equality!* He smiled. So why did his stomach feel funny? He tiptoed back to bed and reread the last two chapters of *Absolutely Fair!*

The sun rose above silence. The rooster slept in; the cows fed just their calves. The hens laid not one egg—the body-conscious among them sensing discomfort ahead. They were too sleepy to pull carts; their string harnesses lay empty beside the hay wagon.

The horses stumbled a cart to town with Theon. Metamorphosing, they felt unreal as horses but not yet secure as poet and musician. Only the graceful sow attended exercise class; the instructors excused themselves for feeling ill after late hours and rich food. Exercising alone on the equipment, Clio remembered routines and corrected her form as best she could.

The apple trees had enjoyed the music and poetry, but still detected no almond or cherry buds.

Theon returned from town with brass tubing and woodcarving tools. He carved a wooden sign—FAIRHAVEN—to fit over the gate, gouging himself only twice. The balance scale weather vane went together nicely and any wind above thirty miles an hour could turn it.

Felicity brought glad news to the chickens: Abigail had recovered and moved to Seattle, where she was very happy.

And the nightclub had been such a great success that she was scheduling one each week for animals to enjoy performing and being entertained. Admission was talent or food. Cows were given front-row seats.

Spring came: time to plow and plant. Theon was afraid to call an all-farm meeting, but he needed cooperation. He had just enough cash for new seeds, but no money coming in from milk, cheese, eggs, or produce. The horses refused to *pull anything*—plow, cart, wagon, sleigh, or carriage. Their identities were completely remade as poet and singer/songwriter. It had taken so long to feel natural in their new roles—only someone who's done it can understand—and so long to establish a public persona that neither would consider retreating.

The hens spoke of nothing but endurance training and power eating. When Theon mentioned eggs, they raged at his stereotypical, patriarchal, obsolete, disenfranchising, limited and limiting thinking. "Horses have always lived best, and we're finally, finally proving that with fair opportunities, we can pull equal loads. Our chickhoods, with unconsciously absorbed limitations, weakened us, but if our generation creates the opportunity, the next generation will pull carriages and sleighs."

Theon told the apple trees they had such awful aphids because they were stressed. And they told him he could start holding good thoughts for almonds and cherries or go live in town.

The cows were svelte and their calves tall and strong. But they remained thick-hoofed and clumsy. They blamed the cat for getting a head start on luxury—all except the heifer with the shiny coat, who'd never produced milk and didn't intend to, who kept her opinions to herself. But they were all eating grass because there was no more hay, corn, or silage. Nor were there fruits or anything requiring a plow. Theon had shoveled a kitchen garden to keep himself in carrots and potatoes, but the overall straps slipping off his bony shoulders were driving him crazy.

The figures in the *County Agricultural Bulletin* said it all: Fairhaven (formerly Dormer Family Farm) had slid from first place to dead last—the least productive farm in the county.

Finally one morning, Theon called an all-farm meeting in the barnyard. No one came.

Felicity, glossier than ever, watched from the barn door-way to see if anyone else attended. Clio sauntered through the barnyard, willing to listen if the meeting was substantive; the other pigs refused to reschedule exercise class, though none but Clio looked slimmer.

Belle and Star were sleeping. Nocturnal creators, they slept until dusk. They still whinnied and reared if any-one laughed near them; they assumed it was a slur on their intelligence.

The chickens, suffering from tendonitis and joint strains, lay under their perches, listening for any references to horses, carts, pulling, draft animals, strength, or power. One hen was missing, Theon noticed. The rooster pulled his fire engine into the farmyard and leaned against it sideways to display his thigh muscles.

Theon cleared his throat. "Even if no one listens, I have to announce that Fairhaven is … not … prospering as a farm. We are engaged in a … noble experiment … absolute fairness for all. But Banker Stan McClosky is coming tomorrow to foreclose on Fairhaven." Theon said more, but his voice was so whispery that no one heard any of it.

The next day, Banker McClosky drove up in a black Mercedes, dust settling on it from the unkempt Fairhaven road. McClosky stepped from his car into ankle-deep grit, and cursed.

"Theon." He reached to shake hands. "This was the top farm in the county, so I know *you're* first-rate. I see your animals here, some a mite skinny"—he nodded at the cows and Clio—"and others not laying. Of course, those trees are diseased. It can't be you. I assume it's climate change or creeping wetlands."

Theon thought, but not fast enough.

McClosky continued, "*I* certainly can't farm; I'm a banker. I have no choice, Theon, but to sell this land to a developer—for a condo village. You have three months before you can be evicted, but the developer's ready to come in here whenever you're ready to sell."

Theon swooned, falling unconscious at the banker's feet.

The cat rushed to lick his face, but decided, instead, to rub against the banker's shin. As McClosky leaned down to brush the cat hair off his trousers and pat Theon back to consciousness, a sheaf of papers slid from his coat pocket. One paper blew away and Felicity pounced on it to help the banker. When she saw the paper closely, however, she scampered and slid to push it behind the barn.

Cornering the barn, Felicity found the paper crunched beneath Clio's front trotters. The pig bent over the handwriting. "Shall we read it together?"

ANIMAL DISPOSAL: the paper began. It listed every Fairhaven inhabitant, with a destination.

Horses—K-9 Diet and Glue Factory

Cows—Snevel's Butcher Shop

Chickens—Bob's Bar-B-Q

Pigs—Bob's Bar-B-Q

Trees—firewood

Cat—pound

"So this is fairness," Clio said. "We'll all be killed."

Felicity batted at a fly. "Not me."

"Not any of us!" Clio said. "Theon and his book got it wrong. Life isn't fair. Life is our chance to find out who we are. I don't want to be *equal*; I want to be *me!*"

Felicity kneaded the floor with her paws. "Stupid experiments. The tradition we overthrow is just the previous experiment."

"But we keep mutations that work," Clio said. "Social evolution."

"Social whiplash." The cat stood up. "You tell the others."

"I will."

Felicity purred. "This is goodbye. Prosper." She gave Clio

a friendly shouldering on her way to the barnyard where Theon was regaining consciousness.

She watched the banker help Theon—awkwardly, red-faced at bending over, his belt too tight. McClosky was an unsmiling man in an expensive suit and exquisite shoes—wearing a wedding ring!

Felicity leaped through the open window of the Mercedes to finish combing her fur behind the driver's seat. Her unique markings might easily be taken for signs of rarity and value. The wife of a spoiled man would need the support of an understanding cat.

When McClosky left, Clio assembled the animals in the apple orchard to read the list. Silence froze the orchard.

"We have three months," Clio said. "We were the best. We can do it again." She looked into faces she knew better than her own.

Wailing and stomping thawed the silence. A hoof thumped Clio's side as cows stampeded past. "Sorry!" someone yelled. Dust choked her, and she closed her eyes.

Hens ran to nests to squeeze out proof of competence, extolling the proteins in eggs. The rooster flew many sharp rocks to the barn roof, vowing to brain McClosky or any henchman who stepped one city shoe on Fairhaven's sacred ground.

The young, smooth cow seduced a neighbor's bull and lured him into her pasture. The apple trees displayed buds they'd been hiding with leaves—secretly awed by their irrepressible gift—and the pigs quit holding their stomachs in.

Theon sharpened the plow and bought new seeds. All the fields had been fallow, so he could plant every acre in spinach, lettuce, carrots, and beets that would sprout fast and earn a fortune.

Belle and Star kept the harness taut and plow straight, walking in rhythm to their poems and songs expressing love for their valley, respect for each other, and observations on envy.

Three months later, when the vegetables were harvested and McClosky was paid in full, Theon shoved *Absolutely Fair!* down the outhouse, where it landed beside *Harnessing Insect Power* and *Building Boats from Banana Leaves.*

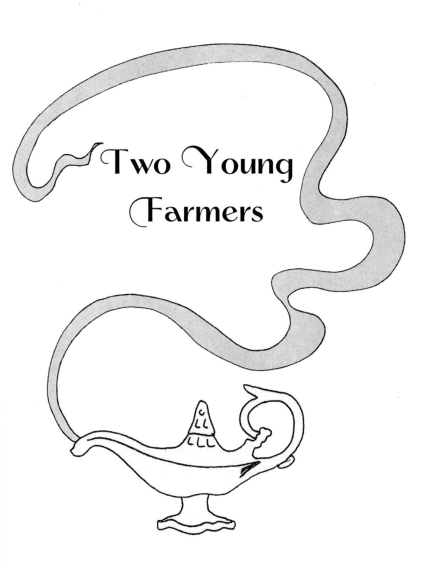

Two Young Farmers

Oone spring, two young men set out to make their fortunes. Garth was tall; Ben was handsome. Each bought a piece of land and built a tiny cabin and a simple barn and corral.

Garth and Ben needed cows, sheep, hens, and pigs, plus seeds, oxen, and plows. Each man took a leather pouch of coins to the local fair.

Garth found a fawn-colored cow with a lovely straight back, strong legs, and a smooth, full udder. Fingering his coins, he walked toward the owner, standing by the cow's head. As Garth approached, however, the cow turned to him, and he saw with shock that she was missing one eye. "She's injured!" he blurted.

"Aye," said the herdsman. "But a gentler, better milker you'll not find at this fair."

"I'll look around."

"Suit yourself." The herdsman brushed a bit of straw from the cow's cheek.

In the next stall, Garth found a fine strong ox, but it had a bent horn. Another large ox had a sore on one leg. Every other bovine was crooked or weak.

At the plowwright's stall, Garth rubbed the plow handles. "Splinters! So crudely finished, they're a disgrace!"

The plowwright grumbled about not having time.

"Here's one split!" Garth said. "That plow's rusted; this handle's loose. I can't use these!" He stalked to the chicken pens, where he found roosters with gnarled toes and hens missing feathers. "Are these sick?" he asked the poultryman.

"They're standing up."

"They're half brown and half black!"

"Don't shout," the poultryman said. "The eggs still hatch if the chickens are pink."

Garth turned in disgust to the pigs. But they were no better. Spotted or small, limping or old, they were poor stock to begin a farm. He walked away to find the sheep.

At last he found a perfect lamb—with a pure black face, creamy wool, dainty black legs, and polished hooves. "How much?" he asked the shepherd.

"This is my prize." The shepherd brushed the lamb's face and pulled at her wool, then patted it smooth. "Her name is Daisy."

"How much is Daisy?"

"Four gold sovereigns."

"Four! Does this wool turn to gold? Does she spin it herself?"

"Three gold and five silver," the shepherd suggested.

"Does she lay eggs and make butter? This is only a lamb, here."

"Don't yell; you'll frighten her," the shepherd said. "How many lambs are you buying?"

"Daisy. The one. This lamb! Are you deaf?"

The shepherd shook his head. "I can't sell you one lamb. Sheep get lonely. I'll give you a deal if you buy a half dozen."

Garth clenched his teeth and his face grew red as he took the coin pouch from his pocket. Carefully, he counted three gold sovereigns and five silver coins into the shepherd's hand, took Daisy's lead into his own, and led her home to his empty barn.

Ben came up the rows behind Garth, carrying three bags of seeds. He found the fawn-colored cow with the straight back, fine legs, full udder, and missing eye. "Lovely cow," he said. "What happened to her eye?"

"Kicked by a horse," said the dairyman, "as a calf. Healed right up, but there she is without the eye." He rubbed the cow behind the ears. "But a gentler, finer milker you'll not find at this fair."

Ben examined the cow from nose to hooves and decided

she was, indeed, the gentlest cow with the most milk at the fair. "How much is she, with the missing eye?"

"Well," said the herdsman, "with both eyes she'd be eight gold sovereigns. With the injured eye … perhaps seven."

Ben and the farmer bargained to six gold pieces, and Ben picked up his seed bags and led the gentle cow behind him, to buy tools and more animals.

At the plowwright's stall, he saw the handles—some splintered, some split. He pulled the handles and pushed the shares. He found a fine plowshare but no decent handles. "I'll buy a plowshare," he told the plowwright, "but you keep the handles."

"I sell them together," the wright said.

"Do you sell any at all?" Ben asked.

The plowwright glowered.

"Better a share than nothing?"

The plowwright cleared his throat.

"Perhaps the blacksmith could make me a plowshare this winter," Ben said.

"One gold piece," the plowwright muttered.

"Two silver," Ben countered.

"Three—no less," said the plowwright. "And keep the handle."

Ben paid him three silver pieces, set the seed bags on his new plow, and dragged it beside his cow to the poultry pens, where Garth was insulting the chickens.

"These chickens look ill," Ben agreed. "A chicken that dies gives neither eggs nor meat, nor wakes me in the morning."

He pulled his cow, seeds, and plow to the pigpens.

The old pigs were cross and the weak ones were lazy, but a small pig in the corner had bright eyes.

"Come out here," Ben called to the pig. "Can you walk?"

The owner set the piglet in front of Ben, where it squealed and snorted, running back and forth.

"If I feed him, he'll only grow bigger," Ben said.

The swineherd nodded.

"Two silver pieces?" Ben asked.

"Seven."

"Two and a copper?"

"Six and nine coppers."

"Two, and two coppers?"

They agreed, before the piglet grew old, on two silver and six copper pieces. Ben put the piglet in a basket and slung him across the cow's back, but she bawled a protest at carrying a piglet.

So Ben found the oxen and saw the scrawny, the lame, and the unmanageable. Then he found the tall oxen, one with a bent horn and one sore-legged. They were very strong and nicely matched. So he bought them for three crowns each and had money left for a sturdy cart and yoke.

He yoked the oxen to the cart; put the piglet, plow, and seeds in the cart; tied the cow behind it; and stopped by the sheep pen on his way out of the fairgrounds.

"A dozen lambs!" the shepherd called. "Wool for winter, mutton for dinner; buy these lambs!"

Some lambs were muddy, some were dusty; most had straw in their wool. Ben pictured the lambs in his grassy meadow away from dust and straw, and washed by rain. "How much for six?"

"You want a dozen?"

"Half a dozen."

"A dozen means I go home tonight. Buy a dozen."

"How much for six?"

"Twelve gold sovereigns for six; fifteen for a dozen."

"Ten gold sovereigns for six?"

"Thirteen for a dozen."

"Thirteen for the dozen." Ben paid the shepherd, put his lambs in the oxcart with his piglet, and went home. He put the cow, lambs, and piglet in the barn for the night, and the oxen in the corral.

The next day Ben hobbled the cow and oxen in his meadow, built a sty for the piglet, and paid a young shepherd to take his dozen lambs with the shepherd's flock to the mountains for the summer. Next Ben cut the crooked horns off one ox and put shiny brass knobs on the stumps, and salved the other ox's sore leg twice a day till it healed. He sanded the splinters off the handle of his plow.

Spring turned to summer, and summer to fall. The leaves fell before the snow, but soon both were thick on the ground. Ben's cow had given milk for cheese and butter, his pig was fat, and his oxen had drawn the plow and cart while the sheep grew wool for next year's sweaters, blankets, and rugs. He traded his extra butter and some pumpkins for a thick new wool sweater and cap.

Ben finished his work early one afternoon and took his fiddle to Garth's to play him a song and invite him to supper. He found Garth looking older than his own father. Garth's hands were callused from breaking soil with a pick instead of a plow. His sunburned face was scratched from hunting wild rabbits in bramble thickets. His teeth were long from no milk or cheese. He was thin and his sweater thinner. Daisy sulked beside the lonely barn.

"Garth!" called Ben. "Will you join me for supper and a song or two?"

Garth straightened up tall and saw Ben's rosy cheeks and fat-yarned sweater. He saw the fiddle case. He looked at his own raveling sweater and faded pants and squinted out at his land, barely used and hardly useful with just one animal and no tools.

Ben called out again, "Will you bring Daisy for a bit of company with my sheep? And you and I'll have roast potatoes and pumpkin pie."

"More!" shouted Garth. "I'll *give* you Daisy and sell you my land—with my cabin, corral, and my barn. I might as well. You got the only good animals at the fair, leaving none for me. I can't make something out of nothing—fairy's wings out of dried leaves. I'm moving to the city, where there are possibilities for a man of standards and ambition!"

Ben stood quietly as Garth's plans settled onto the perfect sheep and evaporated into the dusk before turning orange to join the sunset.

Ben walked toward Daisy, her head drooping, her wool full of burrs. "Aye," he said, scratching gently behind her ears until she lifted her head. "Bring the sheep back to her flock and we'll play a tune before supper. After supper I'll buy your farm."

Ben picked up his fiddle case and beckoned to Daisy and Garth. Gently, he said to Garth, "Good luck in the city."

The
Second-best
Juggler in the
World

A juggler named Ralph kept his eyes open for opportunities. So when an art museum auctioned an ancient bronze oil lamp, he bought it. Unwrapping the lamp and seeing its patina and dents, he felt sure it was authentic—used in a real household, undisturbed since antiquity. His hands trembled as he rubbed it.

A genie with puffy eyes slithered from the spout, cracking his neck and rotating his shoulders. "We're talking *stiff*, here. Stiff! *You* try getting comfortable in that thing for 2,000 years. But I'll get to the point." He aimed a professional smile at Ralph. "In gratitude for freeing me from this curséd lamp,

I hereby grant you two wishes. Anything you want. Within reason."

"*Two*!? Uhhh ... isn't it supposed to be *three* wishes?"

"Who's the expert here? Do I look like a genie?"

"You. Definitely. But isn't it always three?"

"That's the hype. The reality is two."

Ralph cleared his throat and stood up straight before the genie. "For my first wish, I want to be the greatest juggler in the world."

"Aren't you already?"

"Almost. There's a Chinese guy who's awfully good."

The genie shrugged. "You're the juggler; you know who's who. I just hate to see you waste a wish on a one-percent improvement."

"At this level, one percent makes you the best in the world."

The genie reached under his turban to scratch his ear. "These wishes are priceless."

"That's why I bought the lamp!" Ralph nodded warmly to the genie, to smooth their bumpy start.

The genie arched his eyebrows.

Ralph took a deep breath and stood in front of the genie again. "For my first wish, I want to be an ideal husband and father."

"That's two. You want to blow them both at once?"

"Those count separately? My wife and kids are my one family."

The genie crossed his arms. "If I give you a double, I have to give everybody doubles. You see that."

Ralph inhaled carefully and considered. "I would like to be twice as smart!"

"Double your IQ?"

"I can manage our troupe's money, design all our costumes, teach my sons to juggle bigger objects, know what to say to my wife. Twice as smart will do it, and that's one wish."

The genie smiled down his nose. "Those are special talents, not intelligence—designing costumes, managing money, teaching. Smart helps, but without talent, brains are boring."

Ralph studied the genie carefully.

The genie yawned.

"All right. Let's go for a new car."

"You'd waste a once-in-a-lifetime wish on a car you can buy with cash?!"

Ralph put his face in his hands. "I paid a lot for this lamp. Is there a money-back guarantee?"

"Who's going to believe you honestly thought you'd get two magic wishes?"

"Three."

The genie rolled his eyes.

Ralph inhaled until his belt creaked. "Is there a list of approved wishes to choose from?"

"RalphRalphRalph, you can wish for anything you want. It's *your* choice, not mine."

"Then let's just grant me a wish, okay?"

"Absolutely. What do you wish?"

"I wish you'd grant me a damned wish!"

"Bingo. There's your first wish: that I'll grant you one wish. What will it be?"

"You conniving cheat!" Ralph grabbed the genie's throat, but it was only vapor that disappeared where he squeezed. "You're a powerless fake."

"Easy does it," the genie said. "You have one magic wish coming to you. Your neighbors don't have any. You're one hundred percent better off than they are."

Ralph shook his head and stood super straight. "Fine. Let's start again. Lucky me." He wanted excellent health for all three of his sons and his wife, but he knew the genie would count that as four wishes. Their house needed a new roof, but he'd ridicule it. At last he said, "I wish to be wise."

The genie snickered. "Okaaay." He opened his mouth and filled his lungs to blow one enormous breath, *Whh-hooooooooooooouff,* smelling of ancient fish and tarnished bronze. He leaned back, smiling.

Ralph inhaled as much magic air as he could without gagging. Closing his eyes, he focused all his senses on receiving new wisdom. He was ready for anything—a new idea, a feeling of warmth ... special energy. Lights? Sounds? He waited.

He looked into the genie's face for help.

The genie looked away.

Ralph shut his eyes, less confidently.

The genie gnawed a fingernail and spat the chip onto the

floor.

Ralph opened his eyes. "Aren't you supposed to leave when you grant your final wish? Isn't that how it works?"

"It works however we make it work. It's different every time. I want to see what you'll do."

Ralph closed his eyes again, opening his mind and heart as wide as they could stretch, for one last try.

Absolutely nothing.

A stomach ache grew behind Ralph's shirt buttons. *He's a fake. And I bought the lamp.*

The genie hummed in a raspy voice, clapping spasmodically with the song.

Ralph slid his hands up to plug his ears.

"Here's a deal," the genie said. "A DEAL," he yelled, to get Ralph to uncover his ears. "I'll give you an extra wish if I can live in your guest room while I get used to living outside here—making friends, getting a job? A year should do it." He pulled the tail of his vapor from the lamp.

Ralph pictured the genie eating dinner with his wife and children every evening. "No!" He felt the genie's sarcasm stinging their gentle ears. "No!" He plucked the lamp from under the genie and flung it, spinning, high into the air.

"What're you doing?" the genie yelled.

From the table Ralph grabbed five juggling balls and tossed them up with the lamp until all six objects spun a blurry circle higher and higher. "Wise people do what we do best, that we love doing."

When the lamp passed close by, the genie dived into it, and Ralph grabbed it, jamming his handkerchief into the spout. He rewrapped the lamp and returned it to its box—not letting anything rub it—and taped the box shut. He drove it to the art museum and gave it to the woman at the front desk. "You may return this lamp to your basement," he said. "I don't need my money back."

"Is something wrong with it?" she asked.

"Not really. Opportunities aren't guarantees."

"Excuse me?"

"It works however we make it work. It's different every time."

"What?" She stood up and beckoned to a guard.

Ralph smiled at them, walked out the door, and drove home to kiss his wife, hug his sons, and practice juggling.

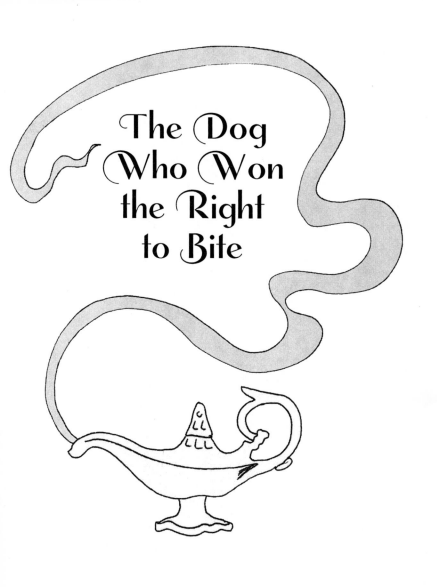

The Dog Who Won the Right to Bite

A huge dog with matted fur ran away from a farmer who was glad to see him go because this dog bit often and hard. The dog settled in the forest, where he soon sniffed out more biting opportunities than ever.

He *loved* to bite. He enjoyed sinking his teeth into flesh and savored the first salty trace of blood. Growling and snarling excited him.

His victims *dreaded* being bitten. They loathed the dog's saliva on their fur or feathers. They were terrified of his teeth probing—then tearing—their skin. The growling and snarling gave them nightmares.

A raccoon and two opossums sued the dog for physical and emotional pain plus loss of livelihood because whenever the dog roamed, they dared not search for food.

The owl sitting as judge was sympathetic to their case, but the dog was defended by a raven who claimed that "Because biting is the nature of the dog, depriving him of the right to bite denies him the civil liberty of being himself."

The foxes filed an *amicus curiae* brief raising the question that if dogs were kept from biting, might owls and all other birds, bats, and insects be barred from flying? Might fishes' swimming be prohibited? "We are never in favor of infringing on any animal's rights, lest it set a precedent for us all."

The owl ruled in favor of the dog. The raccoon and opossums limped away, neither protected nor vindicated, but weakened by the stress of the trial and certain that the dog's previously random aggression was now focused on them. In fact, soon after the trial, the raccoon suffered fatal cardiac arrest when the dog sneaked up behind him and barked.

At the raccoon's funeral, friends whispered that his fur had never been full, nor his eyes bright, after the dog first attacked him. Some eulogized the raccoon for bringing the dog closer to taking responsibility for himself; others muttered, "Lot of good it did him."

Leaving the funeral, animals redesigned their lives: Any animal who could fly, flew—resting and eating only in treetops—coming to ground just for water, in groups, with sentries posted. Burrowing animals dug silently, their food supplies dwindling. Large, hoofed animals traveled only with antlered males and made their young run in the center of the herd, where they breathed dust and couldn't see. Solitary hunters and browsers formed groups and rotated guard duty with stalking and grazing.

The new habits were ridiculously inefficient, causing overgrazing and erosion in some areas while leaving excellent meadows untouched. But they saw no choice. Straight paths grew over with grasses as paws, claws, and hooves wore circuitous new trails deep in the forest, through heavy brush, behind boulders. Animals bent their lives to avoid the dog.

Meanwhile, the dog enjoyed his celebrity. Loathing was not love, but instilling fear shared some elements with inspiring respect. Mostly, though, he was pleased to continue biting because he sincerely, honestly enjoyed it. It *was* his nature to bite.

As ground-nesting birds became scarce, the dog developed a taste for rabbits. Their spines cracked subtly; their haunches were firm between his teeth. Their fleetness made them a challenge, and their sweet natures aroused the dog's scorn. They were a fully satisfying bite.

The animals endured four seasons of the dog's biting whenever he was in the mood. His biting moods became more frequent, and he experimented with new grips to counteract boredom.

But one morning, two jays met for pine nuts. "Ridiculous!" one jay observed. "Flying over this forest, I see animals taking the longest trails to get anywhere."

"We birds are no better," said the other. "Treetops are stripped bare as boulders, while any seed, fruit, or insect that falls to the ground can rot there before we'll risk getting it."

A woodpecker flew up to join them. "We no longer teach our young to fly, but to flee."

The son of the raccoon who lost the court case climbed the tree carefully, one leg and both ears healing from bites. "It makes no sense," he said, "for every one of us to stand guard and take long trails so one dog can roam free and run in straight lines to bite us! All of us together should capture and guard *him*." He looked over his shoulder, from habit.

Hearing voices raised on the dread topic, animals slithered or soared, walked or waded toward the discussion. Soon the surrounding treetops and ground beneath were filled with creatures echoing "Wiser to tie and guard one dog than for five hundred to tie ourselves up dodging him!"

The foxes debated the constitutionality of society's denying a canine his right to bite versus the canine's denying the rabbit his ability to hop.

"It's fine if he's a *dog*," said the young raccoon. "Who here objects to his barking, howling, or having fleas? We simply refuse to let him *bite us*."

"The court has ruled—" began the owl.

"Let his hot breath mat *your* feathers," yelled a squirrel.

144

"And his hard toes trap *your* tail to the ground!"

"Feel his sharp teeth," screamed a badger, "to understand whose rights need protecting!"

A woodpecker drummed for attention. "Where is his family?"

"He bit his littermates!" said the squirrel.

A general growl shook the leaves, then faded.

The jays ruffled their feathers. The raccoon stretched his sore leg.

"We don't want to be extreme," said the woodpecker.

"With my leg and ears, I can't— " said the raccoon.

"We're only birds," said a jay.

"Too small," agreed a woodpecker.

They turned to a mountain lion crouching in a tree. The lioness licked her paw. "As long as I stay to back trails, he doesn't bother me." She added, "I've got cubs."

Silence soaked the trees.

Then the badger leaned forward, whiskers stiff with emotion. "Did *laws* protect us?"

The squirrel leaped to a higher branch and pointed to the young, bloodied raccoon. "Did the court save his father?"

"No," the crowd murmured. "No help at all."

The badger stood up. "We can't sleep, eat, walk in our own woods. This dog's an outsider, anyway."

"He is that," nodded a mouse.

The squirrel beat his fist against the air. "*He* needs to feel pain. Laughing at us! *He* needs to know fear!"

The badger climbed to a better branch and broke off a twig obscuring the crowd's view of him. "Friends," he announced, "we have tried the courts. We have tiptoed around mountains, we're starving, and our young are born into terror—to protect this dog's rights. And he bites more than ever—laughing as he bites!"

The badger looked among the crowd, face by face. "Shall we turn our soft throats to him ... and let him bite? Or shall we turn our sharp claws on him—and hear him squeal?"

"Claws!" yelled the squirrel.

"Fangs!" screamed a bobcat.

"To shreds," howled a wolf.

"No mercy," shrilled the mouse.

The animals flowed down trees and across the forest floor, to a meadow, along a stream, and back into woods, hunting the dog. Their anger built with every snarl. Each hot paw striking the trail focused their rage.

Finding the dog, they fell upon him so ferociously that when birds flew back to their nests and mice scurried home to cold burrows, there was not enough dog fur left to make a hat. And all the animals spent the night scouring their claws—some licking them clean, others scratching theirs dry on bark.

In the morning, a doe led her fawn into meadow grass deep and untouched since the dog's arrival. Rabbits were already there.

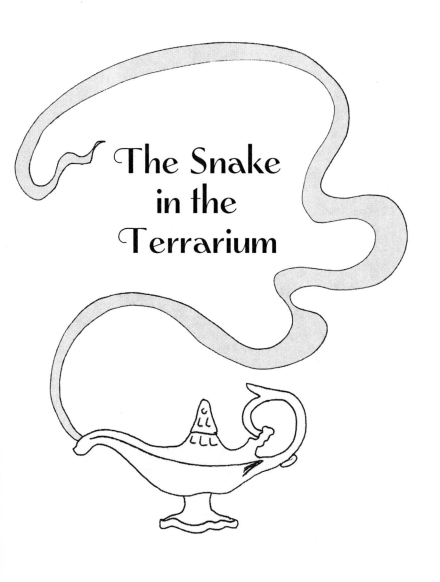

The Snake
in the
Terrarium

A boy caught a gentle striped snake and locked her in a small terrarium.

Trapped in the glass box, the snake slid into misery because she could not stretch her body out straight. She ached; her six hundred and twelve muscles cramped and began to atrophy. She felt her brain shrinking.

Outrage wrestled desperation.

But one morning, the snake awakened with a plan. She nudged all the Repti-litter in her glass box into miniature mountains and tiny valleys. She swam laps in her water dish.

She developed a stretching routine using all eight corners of her wretched cage, and pursued it with discipline every morning and evening. She practiced *capturing* the dead mice her owner fed her. She made herself charming so the boy would take her out of the cage and hold her every day.

At last, one noon, the boy left the terrarium lid poorly latched. The snake—powerful and mostly confident—slithered out of the cage, down the table-leg, and under a door to fresh air, sunlight, and live mice.

The Woman & Her Spring

Awoman bought a log cabin near a spring on the side of a mountain. The spring ran clear and pure all year round because a plug of rock kept the water from gushing out too fast and running away.

At the spring one morning to get water for the day, she noticed the rock plug was loose. Water squirming through the crack around the plug was wriggling into the spring pool. *Oh no!* she thought. *If it isn't one thing, it's another.* But she didn't feel like getting wet and wrestling rocks, so she carried her water bucket home and tidied her cabin.

The next morning, water coursing through the crack

had filled the pool to its lip. "Uh-oh," she said. "I must fix this plug immediately." But she had no idea where to start, let alone any tools. So she went home and baked a birthday cake for her neighbor.

The next day the side of the mountain was spongy as she carried her bucket to the spring. The water had tossed the rock plug down the mountain and was roaring from the hole as though it had someplace important to go. "An emergency!" she cried. "I can't live without this spring!" But she was too scared to even look at it. So she picked a bouquet of flowers for a sick friend.

When she got home, water soaking the floor of her cabin was staining the legs of her chairs and tables. It gave her such a stomachache to see the mess the water was making that she went to bed early and pulled the blankets over her head.

During the night, the mountainside swollen with water slid into the valley—rumbling and crashing—carrying the cabin and the woman with her blankets. They never found a trace of her or even her chimney.

And the spring, without a rock plug or pool, ran wild down the mountain all the way to the sea.

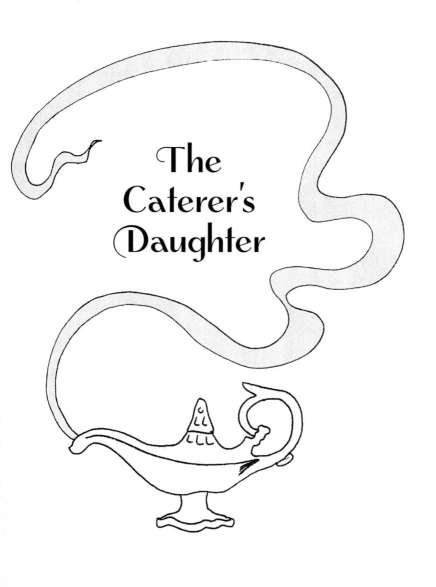

The
Caterer's
Daughter

A caterer named Lola created such delightful parties that the name "Lola" became a verb: "Sir, I believe you can win this election if you *Lola* your Kick-off Dinner."

Everyone recognized Lola—blonde curls above hands rearranging chocolate cakes (Swiss, double dark, and white) among framboise truffles and cappuccino mousses. They knew her laugh because when people praised her aromatic vinaigrettes or perfect salmon robed in exquisite Bearnaise, she laughed.

You would think that Lola, catering galas for mayors,

neurosurgeons, athletes, and corporate chiefs, would give parties of her own. But she bought pasture-raised-chicken eggs even for meringues, butter from a dairy that saved her their Jersey cows' best, and handpicked symmetrical raspberries. Ingredients swallowed her profits, and clients booked the best party nights a year in advance. So all her parties were professional.

Whenever her husband, Samuel, mentioned how hard she worked and how slender the remuneration, she would say, "No artist can work with shoddy materials." But when she worked too long and her legs ached, she wondered if he was right.

Miracle of wonders, after twelve and a half years of thinking maybe they weren't meant to be parents, Lola and Samuel had a baby daughter so beautiful that Lola wanted to name her Ambrosia. Sam insisted on Violet, and Lola knew he was right on this.

Violet was a baby people noticed. She had Lola's golden curls and Sam's warm brown eyes, but it was the way she *moved* that fascinated people — she even waved a rattle beguilingly. By the time she learned to walk, it was clear that her tiny leather shoes were instruments of a miniature muse.

Lola and Sam curled their lives around Violet, taking turns pushing her buggy and singing lullabies. But they were careful not to compete for her affection; after thirteen years, they each knew they'd married the great unadvertised bargain of the century. And Violet was so affectionate there was love to squander.

One evening, while enjoying an especially long cuddle,

Lola caressed her baby's tiny arms, as smooth as pudding, and vowed: "Your life will be easier than mine. Sam's right: I work too hard." She considered what would make an easier life. Violet should have more education, marry a richer man—though Sam was the world's dearest husband—and choose an easier job. So. Good schools. And, being so graceful, she must have dancing lessons. For pleasure, of course, and to swoop through her mansion in silk dresses.

To lay aside money for Violet's education and dancing lessons, Lola took on extra parties. And though she could never make herself use ordinary butter or raspberries, she did begin keeping track of the *favors* that are the backbone of catering. In a slender green notebook Lola listed the names of young dance bands she recommended for celebrity weddings—their Big Breaks—and new ice-carvers and florists she hired to create masterpieces for her parties. "You'll see, Sam," she'd say. "Calling these in will help my profit margin."

"*Do* it," he'd say with his eyebrows, but never with his moustache.

Sam made himself a bedtime story expert, developing a repertoire of family lore and children's classics. He drove Violet to her ballet lessons. He said it was because the lessons were after school, when Lola was making quiches and chocolate roses. But it was really because he and Violet had their own Car Talk Club with silly jokes and intelligent conversation.

Violet watched her mother knead and roll mille-feuille dough into thirty-two layers instead of just sixteen. And when her child was in the kitchen, Lola could stuff and tie twenty quails an hour instead of twelve.

But Lola wrote ballet recitals in violet ink in her calendar and accepted no engagements on those evenings. The week Violet was Sugar Plum Fairy in the Nutcracker, Lola and Sam attended the dress rehearsal and every performance—watching from box seats, loges, aisle seats, and the balcony. Lola turned down $49,785.67 in gross receipts during Nutcracker week, without even knowing the total. Her accountant gave her the figure when he asked if she'd been sick that week.

Lola adored Sam, and Sam cherished Lola—though she worked so many hours that some people wondered. All the time her fingers twisted kimmers and sugared fuibobs, she hummed a song she'd made up. The tune was lilting, with a rhythm she loved working to. The words were partly "Slice it, dice it, frost it, bake—a better life for Violet make ... "

Sam, too, leaned himself toward Violet's future. He worked hard as a barber, and he drove her to special stores like Dancer's World for new toe shoes and leotards. He installed a barre on the long living room wall and put the stereo there so she could practice in the biggest room in the house. Pushing furniture back and forth every day seemed normal after a while.

One afternoon Lola came home to rest before a reception honoring the Prime Minister of England. She stretched out on the couch shoved to the end of the living room. Violet was practicing her part in a *pas de deux.*

Lola tucked a pillow behind her neck and watched Violet

breathing the music. Her toe shoe tips plucked at the floor, then floated above her head as her elbowless arms surged and encircled. As Lola's eyelids relaxed, Violet blurred and didn't touch the floor at all. Her leaps and turns seemed natural for a fairy…

Lola's eyelashes hit her eyebrows. What fairy?! What creature who was no longer her little girl, no school child, no skater on sidewalks? Lola saw, with anguish warping awe, that Violet was not taking dancing lessons to be graceful and pretty, for the pleasure of moving to music. Violet was a *Dancer*.

Violet was not her daughter. She was an artist who would feed and be fed by the world.

Tears filled Lola's eyes. A Dancer has no easy life. All the quiches and trifles and framboises and Bearnaises had been for nothing. In her tears, salmon rose from their platters and swam back to the sea; quail gathered their eggs and flew out the window.

Violet danced on, filled with music, flinging and wafting emotions Lola could not bear to feel but could not stop absorbing.

Lola stayed on the couch, leaving her eyes and ears and heart open. In an hour, when she returned to the Prime Minister's reception, she couldn't sing her catchy song. She had to work in an ordinary rhythm at a normal pace, and her legs ached.

At midnight, she melted her body around Sam's and closed her eyes. But her dreams were so vivid she couldn't tell when she was asleep.

At breakfast, Sam asked if the new toe shoes were breaking in yet, and Lola could hear in their voices that Sam already knew.

In the weeks that followed, Lola came home early some afternoons to watch Violet practice. The beauty and power that came from somewhere in the center of the universe dissolved Lola's shock and marinated her fear into recognition.

Lola asked Sam about recitals and the best teachers and shoes, fine troupes and companies, the politics of winning plum roles. Sam was so proud of Violet that Lola was proud of them both.

Violet joined a major ballet troupe and traveled the world, studying and performing, living to dance and dancing to live. Sam and Lola drove and flew to see her dance, bought tapes of performances they missed, and called relatives and friends when she was on TV.

Lola's song filled her again, and she worked to its rhythm as Violet danced to Tchaikovsky. *Besides,* Lola thought, *she is so lovely, graceful, and full of life that she can marry a wealthy man and have an easier life than mine.* She loved picturing Violet in a mansion, hiring caterers, surrounded by musicians and statues and large paintings and armoires bigger than pianos.

On Violet's twenty-third birthday, she brought home to Lola and Sam ... Romulo, a painter. Of oils, in frames? On easels in studios? Lola gasped! Even Sam looked at Romulo's shoes, splattered with cadmium green and burnt sienna.

A wedding?! A *painter*!? Lola smiled so hard she feared for the enamel crown the dentist had warned her not to grind in her sleep.

Alone, Lola wept. She walked with Sam in the park, and they told how much they loved Violet and how she filled their lives. They talked about how they'd filled their own lives.

Then Sam asked, "Did you see her eyes when she looked at Romulo?"

Lola answered, "And Romulo's face when she walked into the room?"

Home from the park, Lola opened her food-stained green notebook. It was nearly full, with almost no cross-outs. "Sam," she said, "we can't buy her a house or enough silver to have big receptions—maybe just enough silver and china to dine well as a couple. But we can give her a wedding."

"A lovely dress and a wedding," Sam said. "To *them*," he added.

"To *them*," Lola nodded.

In the weeks that followed, she sifted names in her green notebook to find the flamboyant ice-sculptor and the world-famous band whose distinctive sound had enchanted even before they got the incredible drummer. She invited all the florists in town to design centerpieces, boutonnieres, and bridesmaids' bouquets. The most gifted florist, who owed Lola most, created a masterpiece for the bridal bouquet.

Lola called catering company owners who'd begun as her assistants in their teens. She called linen and silver companies and a string quartet who fitted their world tour schedule around the wedding. She reserved a cathedral and its reception halls. She called in chocolate-carvers and meringue-sculptors, praline-bakers and truffle chefs. And she sang so fervently as she cooked that all the experts worked to the rhythm of her song. Nobody's legs ached.

Walking Violet up the aisle, Sam was amazed at his balance and rhythm. The ceremony was touching, and everyone cried except the lovely bride and dashing groom.

Afterwards, doors opened to the great reception hall, where ice sculptures captured light from the candles. Topiary trees and garlands of ferns and roses embraced the room and all the celebrants. White-gloved waiters swirled among them with silver trays of quiches, crystal plates of pâtés, and hand-painted platters of meat sliced thin as stained glass. Breads and rolls of every shape and seed beckoned from tables of cheeses. Tuxedoed bartenders served exotic beverages.

Then the doors opened to the dining hall. Flowers in vases taller than men reached from the tables to the chandeliers. Gold-rimmed china, crystal goblets, and pecan wood chairs with velvet seats welcomed guests to miniature portraits of the wedding couple, at each place, painted by Romulo.

Tuxedoed waiters brought dinners of salmon diabolo and filet mignon with infant carrots, parsley potatoes, and delicate salads.

There were champagne toasts and laughing. Then Lola signaled to open the dessert room. With trumpet fanfare, the doors parted slowly and guests were warmed by the scent and beauty of chocolate rose cakes, truffles and trifles, mousses and meringues, tarts and flans, custards and petits fours, glaces and sorbets—and a wedding cake twenty-three layers tall, covered with wood violets picked by hand. There was more food than all of them together could eat in days, and it was so beautiful that eating it was sacrilege. And sacrament.

The bride and groom cut the first piece of cake and fed each other with golden forks.

And then they danced.

The most delicious wedding cake in the world sat on plates, with forks suspended in air above it, as Violet and Romulo danced their first waltz as man and wife. The tiny muse who'd filled Violet's baby shoes had grown to fill her wedding slippers—and it inspired Romulo and the musicians and all the guests ready to dance and all those eating cake.

Lola, herself, put down her cake knife and danced with Sam.

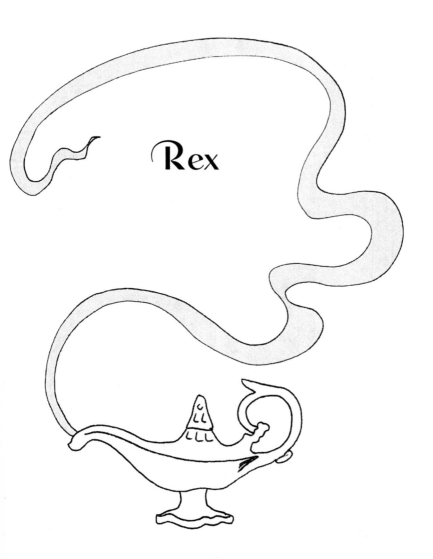

Rex

One Sunday, a teenager named Rex rode with his parents to visit his grandfather in a nursing home. Again this week, Rex let his grandfather call him "Bob" and told him only happy stories about school.

Monday, however, Rex made his friend Monte promise to put him out of his misery if he ever got that old and feeble. "The *stench*," Rex said. "Do you know what a *catheter* is?"

Monte nodded. "The day I can't piss over a pickup truck, come after me with a six-shooter at close range!"

"Grampa's not the worst." Rex whispered, "There's an old lady tied into her wheelchair because she can't sit without falling over. What are these people breathing for? Why do we feed them? Grampa can't want to live like this; he isn't Grampa, anymore!"

Monte shook his head. "That money should paint this school and plug the ozone holes. Those nurses should heal *young* people who can get *well!*"

Neither Rex nor Monte could eat lunch, thinking about it. They agreed to shoot each other at the first tremor or misstep signaling palsy, deafness, blindness, or dementia—any sin of senility.

Rex finished high school, visiting Grampa two Sundays a month, watching him dry and curl into a potato chip. Rex grew proficient at finding reasons to open the window in the stuffy room—to let a fly out, to help his grandfather see spring buds or autumn leaves. Rex's mother always closed it again because Grampa got cold.

Each visit, Grampa's skin would be thinner, his shoulders curled closer to his knees. With horror, Rex noticed that no one was brushing the few teeth his grandfather had left, and moss was growing on them.

In the car on the way home, Rex and his parents would talk about the old days, how Grampa's horse Tyrone had been the smartest equine in the state, able to open barn doors with his nose and corral-gates with his shoulder. They remembered that Grampa had been so tall that it wasn't just good manners that made him remove his hat and bow slightly when he came indoors.

Rex went to college out of state, too far away for Sunday visits. He flew home for Grampa's funeral, where his mother passed around an ancient college graduation photo — a sepia portrait of a dashing fellow with hair slicked back above shadowy eyes, like Rudolph Valentino.

Rex blew his nose. Those were always Grampa's eyes.

They told more stories about Tyrone.

Rex married a girl from college; Monte was his best man. Rex was best man at Monte's wedding, and the two men opened a hardware store.

Children were born and grew. The business flourished, faltered, and flourished again. Children went away to college but worked summers in the store. Monte was quite the investor and let Rex buy him out of the business so he could retire young to California and scuba dive.

One morning when Rex needed a carton of ten-penny nails from a top shelf to fill the customer bulk bin, he asked his son Fred to climb up and get it. "My football knee hates that ladder." Then, as Rex tilted the heavy carton and nails cascaded into the bin, his right shoulder went white-hot weak and he had to finish loading the bin with his left hand. Fortunately, the box was three-quarters empty, so he could do it just fine one-handed.

The doctor said it was a torn rotator cuff, requiring surgery. But it was arthroscopic, so Rex was back at work in a month and just had to avoid lifting until it healed.

Rex did the physical therapy exercises for his shoulder religiously, but he did quit playing tennis. In the pool, he switched to the breaststroke—no more butterfly or crawl—and learned to sidestroke on his left side instead of the right.

When Monte and his wife came back to town for a high school reunion, Rex noticed that Monte's forehead and the backs of his hands had brown spots. And the back of his neck was sun-damaged, with deep wrinkles. Monte's wife, Marie, had had the upper rim of one ear removed for skin cancer. "But they got it all," she told Rex's wife, Elaine, who was showing where she'd had "just a freckle" removed from her cheek because it turned out to be the dangerous kind.

Monte and Marie described their wonderful life in California and invited Rex and Elaine to visit.

Next winter, during peak blizzard season, Rex and Elaine spent a month sunning, swimming, and beach strolling with Monte and Marie. Monte taught Rex to scuba dive.

Before their dive one morning, Monte was downing a handful of pills. "Anti-inflammatory for the old arthritis, then all the junk to keep that from burning a hole in my guts. Hassles, even in Paradise."

"Sure beats blizzards," Rex said.

Carrying scuba masks, tubes, knives, bags, and spear guns, the two friends put on their fins and backed into the surf. They floated at the water's surface, nudged and lifted by swells rolling themselves into waves, as Monte pointed out rock caves, meadows of anemones, and schools of fish. Rex and Monte looked pale green underwater, and Rex felt a thousand mermaids caressing him from mask to flippers. He fought the desire to inhale the whole voluptuous sea.

Monte swam ahead, leading Rex to the best fish. Monte limped in the water—flippered unevenly—and carried his spear gun in his left hand. The arthritis.

Paddling behind Monte, spear gun ready, Rex remembered their youthful promise to never let each other get feeble. Rex doubted Monte could piss over a pickup any more. He hadn't asked.

Monte was hurting; his medication just shifted his pain from arthro to gastro. Rex sighted along his spear gun to a big rock. Then he swung toward Monte—just as Monte looked over his shoulder and motioned for Rex to stop swimming.

Embarrassed, Rex kept arcing the gun past Monte to a small bright garibaldi before tipping it up.

Monte floated a few seconds, his mask a hollow eye staring at Rex; then pointed to a sea lion five yards ahead.

The sea lion rolled and dove intricate figures around them until, looking bored with their inability to play, it dissolved into deeper water.

A wave swelled toward them, brushing all Rex's body

hairs at once and reviving the mermaid sensation; he exhaled a thousand bubbles to avoid exploding with joy. They were *floating* in a *color*—exquisite pale green. What an enormous, foolish loss it would be to give up all this simply because one couldn't discharge a bodily fluid over a vehicle. Anyway, since his shoulder surgery—even arthroscopic—Rex doubted he could stretch the spear gun's rubber sling far enough to fulfill their youthful promise.

He shifted his spear gun and blew out his scuba tube. On the sandy floor of a small canyon was the telltale outline of a large halibut, perfect for the barbecue. But Rex didn't turn his back on Monte, who knew, after all, his shoulder and knee details.

The barbecued fish was divine, and in a few days, Rex and Elaine flew back to the store, grandchildren, dog, and lousy weather. Whenever it was slow in the store, Rex closed his eyes to feel seawater surging over his body like a thousand mermaids.

During the next few winters, Rex had more encounters with his surgeon to ream clogs, snip excesses, and replace parts worn through.

He retired from the store and discovered how much he liked watching flames that filled the fireplace. Relaxing in his leather chair, controlling the angles so his view of the flames was nice and straight but he didn't singe the footstool, he pondered championship football games he'd played, mountains he'd climbed, horses he'd ridden, women he'd loved—some up close, others from afar—and money he'd almost made in the stock market. In his leather chair, he reran winning touchdowns with no need to ice shin splints. Horses grew taller and faster by the month and never needed currying. Women grew fuller-bosomed and fairer-haired with each log piled on the embers and wanted nothing so much as Rex's happiness.

He was wise to remember those women and horses because with his trifocals he couldn't catch the details on new ones. Anyway, the love, thrills, pride, and risks were more precious now that they could never be surpassed. Except that in his long-range view, Elaine's tender loyalty shouldered aside images of fuller-lipped women with cascading curls. "Elaine," Rex would say, "I was awfully smart, awfully young, to find you. Are you my dearest?"

And Elaine would hold him by the ears and kiss him all over the face till he could scarcely breathe.

One humid afternoon Marie called from California. Monte had suffered a heart attack. Could they come to a funeral Tuesday?

A year later, Rex awoke in a room that was definitely not his own. The men there said their names were "Fred" and

"Steve," not "Monte." The women answered to "Elaine" or "Marie," even though they'd told him some other names. There was a familiar-looking tennager who kept opening the window, but one of the Elaines kept closing it.

He smiled at them all, so pleased they'd brought flowers. His smile felt funny on his right side, and when he tried to grab the bed-rail to sit up, nothing happened. So, pushing off with his left arm, he rolled himself to the right, straining his nose toward the flowers, sniffing deeply.

Oh, a florist's bouquet—smelling like every flower in the shop, that glorious, unreal blend of all the world's blossoms! A big bouquet, with its own vase and ferns and a ribbon, and curly doodads sprouting out of the middle.

Rex scanned the room again. Was it his birthday? Or one of theirs? Well. Whatever the occasion, he was truly pleased to be included.

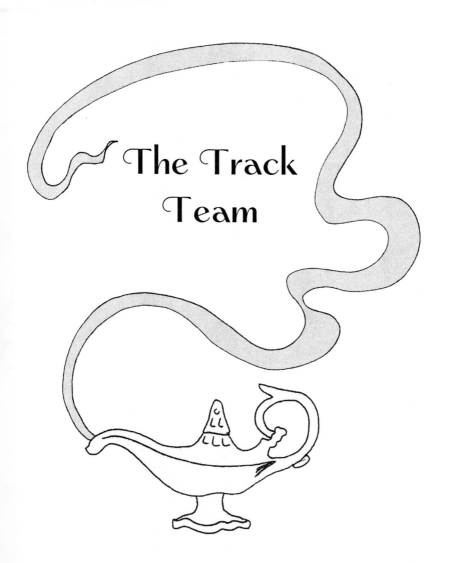

The Track
Team

Three Mt. Pelier High School Wolverines—a sprinter, a hurdler, and a miler—were talking after a track meet.

"This is the *worst* team in the league," groused the sprinter. "I psyche myself out just putting on my uniform."

"Wolverines never *win*," the hurdler snorted, "but didn't we used to put up a fight?"

"When my dad went to Mt. Pelier, Wolverines spread terror. But that was twenty-five years ago," the miler fumed.

The hurdler stretched his legs. "No one tries to beat us, anymore; they try to *lap* us."

The sprinter leaned forward. "You know what we have to *do*, don't you?"

"Well, *I* do!" the hurdler said.

"No doubt about it!" said the miler.

"Yeah," the sprinter said. "We have no choice."

They grabbed their sports bags and climbed on the team bus back to Mt. Pelier.

At dinner that evening, the sprinter cleared his throat and gathered his family's attention. "Uh, Dad, Mom—I'm quitting track." He waited.

No one said anything, so he filled the silence. "Our coach is incompetent, the other sprinters don't practice, we're at the bottom of the league, and every meet is humiliation. It's not like I'm Olympic material. So I'd rather just study or go out more."

His parents looked at him carefully, to see what he wanted them to say.

"It's just—well, I'm not great at it, anyway."

They mumbled supportive condolences, and his sister asked if she could have his sports bag.

The hurdler followed his mother's trail—briefcase, suit jacket, high heels, sunglasses, and car keys—into the kitchen. His mother was dialing, by heart, the Chinese restaurant that delivered. "Mom," he said in his most earnest voice. "You've always taught me to do my best. And we do our best with the right tools. Right? In the right setting?"

She hung up the telephone and turned to face him. She'd known him sixteen years, after all.

"I need a car of my own because I have to transfer to Uni High."

She gave a small involuntary squeal, then crossed her arms and listened.

"I've given it a lot of thought, and all the guys in track agree: Coach Linton is incompetent. He's training us to be losers. It'll affect us for *life* to experience defeat and humiliation week after week. Coach Russo at Uni specializes in technique. He knows what he's doing, and he cares. You've got to help me, Mom."

He stood as tall as he could without looking stiff.

"There's a lot to think about," she said, unfastening heavy earrings. "Uni High, huh?"

The miler was late for dinner, and his father was preparing to bluster, when something in his son's red face stopped him.

"Sorry I'm late, Dad." The miler dumped a stack of books on the table by his plate and left to wash his hands. When he returned, he served himself some coagulated lasagna and soggy salad.

"Look at these, Dad." He lifted the books one by one. "Here's the *AAF/CIF Track and Field Coaches' Program For High School* I got from Coach Linton. This is Jim Ryun's biography. Here's that new book by the physiologist who claims she can cut seconds off runners' times by eliminating inefficiency. And here's my new training schedule; I'll modify it after I read these."

He turned a clipboard so his father could read it. "I can do wind-sprints up our hill. That's why I'm late—I did just one today, because of the meet. And I'm going to ask Coach Rimlay at the college to watch me and give me tips."

He ate some lasagna. "The Wolverines are awful."

"Not all of them," his father said.

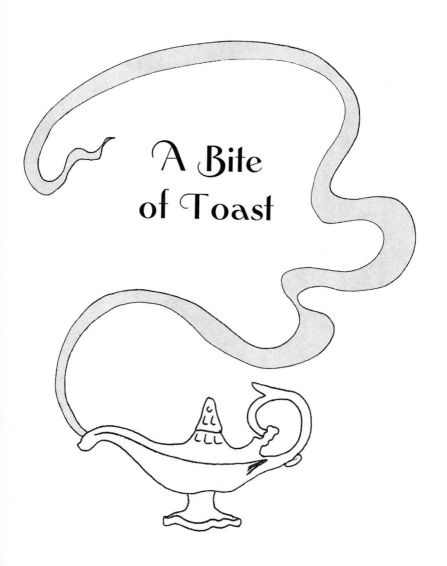

A Bite
of Toast

O ne morning a man thought his wife took a bite of his toast while he was reading the paper. When he picked up the toast, there it was—a bite gone, just the size of his wife's little teeth.

Germs! thought the man. "Nerve!" he said. "You wouldn't do that to the president!"

She showed him the great crumbling crack across the loaf that made all the bread lose a corner in the shape of a bite. He didn't believe her; he chewed the hurt with the rest of his toast.

The hurt filled his mouth and pulled the corners down

hard, thinning his lips. It seeped up into his eyes and puffed them as an allergy would—bags on the bottom and poufs on top till his eyes were red slits.

The man swallowed his hurt, and as it slid downward through his throat it made his neck cords stand out like flag-pole cables. As it soaked into his chest, he pulled his shoulders forward to contain his rage. Silently the hurt bathed his heart, engorging it with purple blood; squeezed his lungs; and bur-rowed into his stomach, from which it loosed acid upon his pancreas and liver. The hurt, floating on the acid, flowed into his intestines; then swelled his legs.

The hurt was toxic now, mixed with stomach acid and purple blood. The man puffed up like a bird in a dust bath, and his wife was alarmed.

"Dovey!" she said. "Is it still the toast?"

Dovey glared through his eye slits and pulled his lips tight so the hurt would not escape.

"How about a cup of tea? A back rub?" she asked.

Dovey swelled and purpled till he could scarcely walk and certainly not talk.

He had done this before, so his wife tried not to worry. But this time the hurt saturated—then unspiraled—his DNA. And that was too much. Only one week after his toast was not bitten, the man was so swollen and purple with nurtured rage that he exploded. He died all over his house simultaneously, and they had to scrape for days to find enough to bury.

~ Epilogue ~

While she was scraping, Dovey's little wife noticed that, even with speckled walls, the house seemed larger and sunnier.

In the months that followed, she let her hair grow into ringlets, and nobody laughed. She bought caramel leather safari boots, and nobody criticized. She took mambo lessons, and partners danced with her.

When the handsome Loan Officer at National Federal Bank asked her to marry him, she accepted his ring—but invited him over for breakfast. She actually bit corners off two slices of his toast, leaving dainty, curved tooth prints in the boysenberry jam. She waited.

"Well," he said, "thank you for making sure the jam is fresh. Shall I sip your orange juice?"

She smiled. "Any morning you'd like."

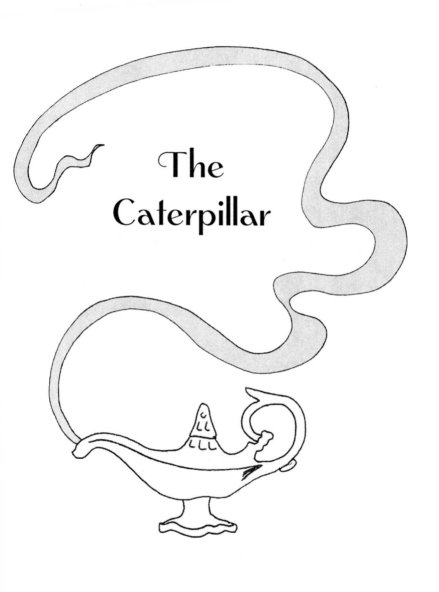

The Caterpillar

There was once a caterpillar with exquisite taste. Her delicate green skin was embellished with one row of white dots, each dot encircled by a perfect scarlet ring.

Even when no one was watching, she held her head erect and extended her dainty feet in steps precisely the same length, to ripple and arch along branches as smoothly as waves rolling to shore. She nibbled just the tender leaves at the tips of branches, avoiding any that curled or bore brown spots or thick veins. She grew long and elegant.

The season came, as seasons do, when the caterpillar yearned to spin a cocoon. She was confident she'd spin superbly, so she focused—as one must for a residence—on location.

It should be out of mischief's reach, she reasoned, but not so high as to blow away in strong winds. Near the end of a branch, beyond coarse bark, but not at a tip that might whip violently in storms. She searched.

As nighttime temperatures dropped, her urgency increased. The trees turned color, and fewer really delicate leaves tempted a discerning palate. She began skipping lunches to site-hunt.

More and more often, rippling up and gliding down trees, searching, she found fresh white capsules already woven by acquaintances. Many clustered in the same trees. It seemed to her that trees chosen by so very *many* might have a common, even vulgar, appeal.

She found a tree with no cocoons. Smooth-barked and clean, it had substantial branches. She liked the tree and had located three lovely sites when it struck her that no other caterpillars had chosen this tree. Though she'd lived brilliantly to this point, there remained the possibility of original error. Doubt chafed her pale rose brain; anxiety furrowed her smooth green brow as she turned downward. She could find a better tree.

Cocoons now hung from house eaves and fence rails. Leaves deepening on the ground made it more difficult each day to walk from tree to tree, even if one maintained no standards at all in stretching forward and regrouping gracefully. But the caterpillar's exceptional breeding—and stamina and determination—enabled her to continue without sacrificing form.

There was some small panic in her searching now, but she hid it. The more anxiety gnawed her, the more she guarded against deterioration the distance between her steps, the height she lifted her tiny feet, the arch of her smooth neck. The more she feared never finding a suitable spot, the more she criticized each location.

At last the caterpillar vowed to choose the next decent place; the nights were too cold, and there was nothing to eat. She pranced doggedly up the tree she'd rejected weeks before because no one else had chosen it. As she struggled among the twisting leaves, dozens of cocoons hung like silken mummies from the smooth amber bark she had admired.

But she was light-headed, uncertain which cocoons hung from the branches and which were suspended in her mind. She stood among the silent comrades sharing metamorphosis, and a desire to join them overwhelmed her. She reached out to one with her head, but he couldn't know and didn't respond.

The exquisite caterpillar clutched the branch with all her dainty feet and readied her spinning mouthparts to make a filament for the base of her cocoon. Her spinneret was stiff and spun uneven filament that wouldn't bond. She was exhausted, afraid of fainting. She clung to the branch and *willed* body fluids into her spinneret.

At last a sticky white liquid oozed onto her spinning parts; she sensed triumph, shaping the ooze into a glistening, even strand. She would spin a perfect cocoon, with smoother, more translucent walls than any of the others. But she would start a new base higher on the branch, above the others. This first pad was uneven, imperfect.

The caterpillar arched her neck, lifting her feet precisely, moving toward the very best location. She stretched and pulled up, glided and rippled in consummate form, to the most desirable place.

She opened her spinneret oozing silver-white silk to weave the perfect base for her ideal cocoon. She dipped her head from side to side in figure eights, turning and swooping as the silk spilled from her jaws, turning and returning, weaving and reweaving, spinning and respinning ... until faintness came upon her with such force that her head rolled sideways, her feet shuddered loose from the branch, and she fell to the end of her perfect thread.

She hung quietly, turning around and around—then twirling back again as the silk untwisted—until it, even in its perfection, broke, and dropped her to the ground.

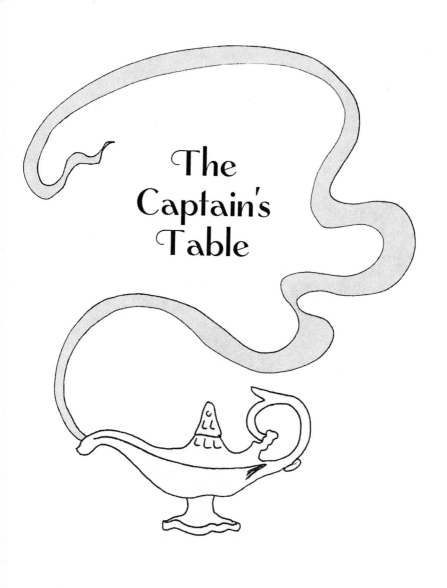

The
Captain's
Table

A dynamic woman named Fiona took a cruise vacation on a large white ship. The *Spirit of the Tropics* offered snorkeling, island-hopping to native villages, and serenades by the crew.

In cotton cruise ensembles with Italian sandals—or designer sportswear with high-tech shoes—she vacationed diligently: fast laps in the ship's pool before breakfast, running up volcano trails, and memorizing polite phrases in indigenous languages.

In swimming pool water-volleyball games, Fiona slid into the back row of demoralized teams; her powerful serves let losers taste sweet victory. She gave impromptu drawing lessons to children and sang harmony with island musicians.

She developed a particular taste for running by moonlight on the main deck, which was fortunate because one midnight a thunderous explosion blasted the *Spirit* into a million slivers of fiberglass and teak. Fiona was blown off deck into the warm tropical sea.

Looking about her in the moonlight, she could see there would be no orderly rescue by the crew because there was neither crew nor lifeboat. There were, however, useful bits of flotsam. She kicked off her shoes and swam to the largest—the captain's dining table, floating upside down. When plastic bottles of Evian water bobbed past, she began to feel lucky. As puffy foil bags of snacks from the bar popped to the surface, she looked around for someone to share her good fortune.

No one. She floated and hoped, called out and listened.

The only answer was seawater slapping the captain's table. It was eerie … appropriate for a respectful ceremony for the many lost. She created one that blended religions and focused on boundless rewards for lives well lived.

Her life lay, thank heavens, in her own two capable hands. Without flares or radio equipment, survival dangled from her ability to swim to solid ground.

She mentally gridded the wreck area: life jackets and swim fins rose and dipped on swells; she put on the very nicest. She harvested tubes of sunscreen and a piece of canvas to shade her tabletop when the sun came up.

On the horizon loomed her ship's island destination; the current rippled toward it. She lashed her provisions to the table legs with flotsal shreds, aimed the table at the island, and began kicking. Breathing evenly and deeply, loose-muscled to squander no strength on muscle tension, she pushed her table through the water.

A mantra buoyed her: "Just *swim!*" She longed to whistle or hum it, but that would've cost energy and compromised breathing.

A thousand kicks later, her legs were stone. Instead of slicing water, they clubbed each other. Luckily, her feet and ankles were numb.

"So it's water-break time!" She sipped Evian more carefully than Chateaux Lafite-Rothschild '47, floating to relax her legs in a sea that supported a horizontal leg but offered no floor to a vertical one.

Her life jacket, overly buoyant, was choking her. She yanked it down and tightened the waist strap before selecting Snack #1, a gold foil bag of Lo-Salt Pretzels. "Carbs and electrolytes for the endurance swimmer."

The moon was a spectacular, if distant, companion. She shooed the fear it could be her last. Shimmying lactic acid from her arms and legs, she took three enormous diaphragmatic breaths and vowed to write her childhood swimming coach a thank-you note the minute she got home.

Pushing the table with straight arms, she alternated frog kicks with flutter kicks to delay cramping. The life jacket added drag, but it allowed spontaneous Breather Breaks between her quarter-hourly Dry-and-Nibble Respites on the raft.

Fiona's self-discipline shrank the ocean. Once each hour, by her waterproof watch, she re-estimated the distance and time to the island.

As the sky lightened, she scheduled a Dry-and-Doze under the canvas, with honey roasted peanuts for breakfast. She put on fresh sunblock and finished a water bottle. Could she put a note in it? No pen, pencil, or plain paper to poke an SOS in, with an earring post. No ships or planes in any direction. "It is wiser," she coached herself, "to swim than to wait for rescue."

When the sun awoke on the horizon, she slid into the water and melted her stiffness by pushing the table forward, proud of her focus and courage where others might dither and drown.

As the sun bored through the sky, Fiona drilled the sea, concentrating on loose, efficient muscles, visualizing shore just a few easy strokes away. And raspberry tea.

Hours passed wetly. Thinking her mantra, she flailed on. Then she heard herself mutter it: "Struggle—or die!"

A swell of seawater filled her mouth. Treading water, she coughed brine and closed her eyes, turning away from the sun's glare on the water.

But treading water let panic catch up.

She jutted her chin to the sun, "The cruise brochure promised adventures!" She forced her face into a smile, crinkling her eyes and dimpling her cheeks. "Ha! Ha-ha, Ha-ha-*ha*-ha-ha!" Keeping the smile in place, she felt for endorphins. All that research on smiling couldn't be wrong.

She dog-paddled the table forward—then *climbed* through the water until her legs locked solid. Refusing to panic, she dragged herself aboard and announced a *Double* Dry-off, with an early dinner and nap under the canvas, while visualizing a powerful hydrodynamic body. "I *am* prioritized," she said. Her eyes closed before she finished a bag of roasted almonds.

When the sun settled into the sea, anxiety awakened Fiona. Was the sea different—or just dark? Was that a shark fin—or seaweed? She scanned for danger, hoping to find none.

Making progress calmed her, so she tumbled into the water and aimed the table directly at the island, kicking and breathing as evenly as she could. But her best was no longer even. She forced her chin above water, her burning eyes open. Her torso churned sideways, wasting momentum and defeating her kick.

"Never give up!" she gasped.

She kicked to that rhythm: Ne-ver gi-vup, ne-ver gi-vup…Out of troughs and over swells, kicking and pushing—was this her millionth trough?

Then, without her permission, her body began sobbing

so violently and yet so weakly that her arms and legs quit pushing and kicking. She was a land animal in an ocean, a human with no tribe. No one who could help her knew where she was. And it was dark.

Fiona cried a shrill keen of self-pity—with no apology. She whimpered. Her crying scared her because it was appropriate.

She tried to hug her table. She stroked her water bottles, caressed a package of macadamia nuts, ran her hand beneath the canvas. The poignancy—and futility—of her preparations, her spirit and ingenuity, her courage and ferocity, made her weep.

"I *did* swim," she whispered ... and felt betrayed.

Through her tears, the island looked no closer. Her arms and legs were already dead, her neck so stiff she couldn't feel it.

"You win—somebody!" she wailed. "I did swim forward, but I did not get there." Words bubbled up out of her chest—she could feel them coming—words she'd thought she would never say: "*I ... give ... up!*"

Her white-stalk fingers clung to the table.

Deliberately, slowly, she let go of it and rolled onto her back. Closing her eyes, she inhaled—ready to breathe whatever filled her nostrils, prepared to sink and drown. She surrendered head and body, arms and legs to the sea.

She floated with arms and legs flung out from her lifejacketed body. The water rocked her gently. Her breathing slowed and deepened; her muscles gave up their cramps, inch by inch ...

She opened her eyes in the darkness, cringing in case a wave rolled over her.

The stars were out ... more than she'd known existed. *Resolutely* there. Bright, distinct. Planets, too, surely. Southern Cross and Milky Way. Perhaps The Gallant Heroine With Flowing Gown and Diamond-studded Sword. The Golden Retriever and Puppies? The sky was a jeweled dome above her and the deep, flat sea.

She felt her hair drying against her face, heard herself breathing. Tilting her hands upward in the moonlight, she studied their backs and fronts like the hands of a stranger. They were water-creped and small, but competent and earnest. Her thumbnails looked like her Uncle Bob's.

She lifted her head to see where she was. A bright yellow fish leaped from the water and flashed away. Beside her floated a piece of seaweed ten feet long—or an animal disguised as seaweed. It might be an ancient creature considered extinct and she'd be the only human to know it still lived. Its edges had minuscule teeth.

Was it waiting to eat her? If a prehistoric predator digested her into molecules then atoms, would *she* become *ancient*?

She rolled upright to poke her stalker.

It bulged away from her; then regained its limber curves.

"Plant." She relaxed into the water.

The seaweed dipped and arched in unison with its supporting water like ice dancers skating together until their muscles act on each other's thoughts.

"I am a *creature*," she said finally, "with atoms as ancient as any. This is not my *medium*, but this is my *world*." She drifted beside the seaweed, supported by her life jacket as the seaweed was buoyed by its little brown air bladders.

Suddenly, she was hungry.

The captain's table floated nearby. She swam to it, climbed aboard, and opened a bag of macadamias and a bottle of water. She stretched out on the table, tucking an Evian bottle under her neck. In the balmy night air, she stopped shivering.

A breeze lifted her hair and stroked her face as tears filled her eyes. For the first time on her vacation, she relaxed.

A lone sea bird flew overhead. Fiona waved.

It was very odd to lie on an upside-down table with no appointments, messages, bills, parties, classes, or meetings. She examined her hands again—then her feet, knees, and elbows. She yearned for a mirror to see her face.

She stroked the water. Silky. She'd always planned to live in a house overlooking the sea, but had never done it. She petted the water. It dipped away from her hand and slapped the table.

As the sun rose, Fiona could see the beach of her island destination. White coral sand flanked knobby green hilltops and clusters of palm-thatched houses. The sea was glassy smooth—too lovely to disturb by swimming. Fronds of pale green seaweed floated in the water, tiny balls edging their stems. She sat up straight to watch them. Petals strewn before a bride.

The wind tapestried the water into a million points, all facing the island, then flattened the water into plaid. Among garlands of seaweed, long white sun splinters pierced the blue water, reaching for the sea floor.

She held her canvas out wide to shade herself from the sun. The wind knew just what to do with it.

During the morning, she ate almonds and drank two bottles of water and watched coral reefs rise beneath the table, then fall away to canyons. Flying fish glinted along the surface. Reef fish of startling blues, yellows, and black swam to her table. She slid a hand into the water; the fish would touch but not be touched.

Her table caught on a coral reef until the next surge lifted it free. The sea deepened again to darker blue, then shallowed to turquoise and finally to palest green.

She stuffed bottles of water and packages of nuts inside her shirt.

When the table wedged itself among the coral and tilted her off into the water, Fiona settled into the sea and floated. She waited for a swell—and kicked within it—helping the water carry her to warm sand that caked her hands and then her feet, welcoming her ashore.

About the Author

Margaret Harmon's award-winning humor and fiction appear in national publications and on public radio. She is the author-illustrator of *The Man Who Learned to Walk In Shoes That Pinch: Contemporary Fables* and *A Field Guide to North American Birders: A Parody*. She lives in San Diego with her husband. For the latest information, please visit her website at:

MARGARETHARMON.COM

CPSIA information can be obtained at www.ICGtesting.com
Printed in the USA
LVOW08s0015060813

346333LV00002B/2/P